TIGHT

tīt/ adjective

Alessandra Torre

ISBN: 978-1-940941-59-2

Editor: Madison Seidler
Proofreader: Jonathan Rodriguez, Perla Calas & Janice Berry
Front Cover Design: Judi Perkins
Back Cover Design: Miguel Kilantang Jr.
Cover Image: Maksim Gorbunov
Interior Design: Bob Houston eBook Formatting

TIGHT

tīt/ adjective

Alessandra Torre

This book is a bit different than my others.
It doesn't follow quite the same formula.
It will take you to some edges, but I don't push you over.

Promise.

Note:

This book was inspired by "Still," a novella in the *Bend Anthology*, which was banned from Kindle in May 2014. Many of the initial Brett/Riley scenes in this book came from that novella. If they seem familiar, that is why.

To Joey.

You are in every hero.

Our love in every story.

chapter 1

6 months before

tight (tīt)
(adj.) close-fitting, especially uncomfortably so.

I didn't belong there—not in a loud casino, smoke curling up the walls, disappearing into discreet vents. Flip-flops shared space with sequins and diamonds, the crowd a mix of sandy tourists and high rollers, eighteen-year-old spring breakers polka-dotting the mix with their wide eyes and slurred steps, the alcohol hitting their virgin systems hard. We were at a craps table, a game that none of us understood, yet the Asians to our right were grinning and gesturing like we were hitting the mother lode, so we blew on dice and moved markers, and our chip stack continued to grow.

Chelsea. She's the reason we were all there. Six of us split between three rooms, the four hundred dollar nightly rate generously taken care of by Mr. McCrory, Chelsea's father and the king of the Atlanta carwash market. Chelsea's big day was two weeks away, so there we were, in Nassau, bachelorette-partying our country asses off.

I didn't belong there. I belonged on my front porch, sunning my toes on the railing, a sweet tea next to me, a magazine on my lap, Sugarland on the radio. That was how I'd spend a week off. Not in that loud place, with Tammy's hand digging into my shoulders, her fresh manicure biting imprints into my sunburned skin. There was a bump of bodies behind me, and the curve of the table cut into my still-gorged-on-seafood stomach. *Ouch.* I gazed longingly at the stool holding up the cigarette-smoking female to my right. My feet were on fire, four hours in a-size-too-small-but-they-were-on-sale heels taking their toll in the most painful way possible.

I gathered my chips and turned to Megan, the bit of a girl to my left, her platinum curls bouncing excitedly at some aspect of this gamble that we didn't understand. "I'm gonna head upstairs," I yelled, my mouth as close to her ear as I could manage without swallowing her chandelier earrings.

"What?" She glanced down at her wrist, the fake Rolex we all—with the exception of Chelsea—had gobbled up from the first roadside stand where the taxi driver had stopped. It glittered impressively at me, and I fought a glimpse downward to see if my own looked as good. "It's only ten."

"My feet are killing me."

She looked down. "You got a long way to walk to the room."

She wasn't kidding. My brain groaned at the thought of the trek before me. Through the casino, through the shops, down a flight of stairs, through a second lobby, up twelve floors via elevator, and then down a thousand feet of hallway. "I know. That's why I'm leaving while my soles still have a little bit of life left in them."

She leaned in, lowering her voice. "Chelsea will be pissed."

I shrugged, craning my neck till I saw the future bride's over-highlighted head. I leaned in, gave Megan a quick peck on the cheek, then hobbled over to Chelsea. "I'm heading up to the room," I called out.

She waved her hand dismissively, her eyes glued to the table, the movement of our Asian coaching staff leaping in the air dominated her attention, her own voice whooped at an ear-splitting crescendo.

Great. I moved before my words registered and her attention changed to me, weaving through crowds of people as fast as my raw feet would take me, opening my purse and dumping my handful of chips into it.

Past blackjack. I could do this. It wasn't really that bad if I didn't pause long enough for my feet to bitch.

Past poker. Damn, there were a lot of tables. I kept my eyes focused forward, like I did when I felt like I would faint. Step, hobble. Step, hobble. I could do this, as long as I was going the right way.

Past more blackjack. Crap. Were these the same tables I passed before? Or different ones? Maybe the others were in a high-roller portion of the casino. These must be different. They had to be different. I looked for a sign, an arrow, a member of the casino staff. The blister on the back of my right heel was now competing with my left pinky toe, which I'd be willing to bet was bleeding.

Past slots. This had to be right. I was jostled out of place by an overweight white woman who shot me a dirty look. Almost turned my ankle and busted my ass. Great. Just what I needed. An injury to accompany my pansy-ass feet.

There was an exit before me, and I craned to see over the heads blocking my view. Please lead out of the casino. Please lead into the lobby by the shops, please ... Oh, thank God. I almost cried with relief when the crowd parted, and I entered the smoke-free arena that was the rest of the hotel. Bathrooms to my left, a seating area on my right. I walked like my ninety-year-old grandma and collapsed into the closest chair, working off my heels with trembling fingers, and moaned when the heavy stilettos dropped to the tiled floor. Sweet Jesus. I flexed my feet and leaned back in the chair, closed my eyes and covered my face for a moment, rubbing gentle patterns into my hairline as I tried to massage away the headache that had built over the last two hours. Aspirin. I'd get to the room, take aspirin, and draw a bath. Soak my feet and create enough bubbles to make Mr. Clean jealous. The prospect brought a smile to my face, and I let my hands drop. Took a moment to breathe, to relax.

Finally, it was quieter, away from the madness of the casino.

I couldn't believe it was only Friday. I got off early, our bank manager unhappy with the request, yet unable to bitch too loudly, seeing as I was the only FA at our small town chain. FA is fancy country talk for Financial Advisor. In a big city I'd manage large portfolios, dispense stock advice, buy and sell quotients like Ben Affleck in *Boiler Room*. But in our small town? Four hour from Atlanta, where Sunday sermons focus on rain prayers, and where the average household income lay right on the forty-five thousand dollar mark? My days were spent selling mutual funds, life insurance, and doing the I'm-not-qualified-for-this job of will creation and estate planning. Nothing that couldn't wait till Monday morning, when my raw feet and hung over self would crack open the doors of Smith Bank & Trust at the ungodly hour of 7:30 AM.

I picked up my right foot and examined the damage done by my stilettos. Stilettos that were uglier by the minute, trotting their pretty selves straight into my trashcan at their current rate of travel. Too bad I didn't pack many other options. Fancy shoes took up a very small corner of my closet. Sensible black grandma heels dominated the rest of said closet floor. Paired with my tan nylons, they helped to complete the too-sexy-for-a-date vibe that I rocked ninety percent of the year. Maybe I couldn't pull off the cute strappy heels, sexpot in a minidress look. Maybe that ability set sail at age thirty. Maybe, at thirty-two, I should invest in some ballet flats and sundresses. I saw a lot of the minivan moms with that look. And they looked comfortable. They certainly didn't have the fire engine red feet that were currently screaming a slow death beneath my fingertips. I gingerly pushed on the bubble on my back heel. Uck. I could almost hear liquid squishing in it.

White fuzziness. It was thrust in my line of vision, interrupting my new fascination with the chipped polish on my big toe. I focused on the white, fluffy soft slippers coming into view. Thick ones, where you'd sink an inch into a pillow top bed of comfort, a brand I'd never heard of embroidered along the top. I looked from the shoes, up a tan arm, my eyes tripping and already drooling over clean nails, a strong hand, a Rolex ten times more authentic than mine, a muscular forearm, rolled sleeves, a jaw I'd nibble to death, and a face that competed with easy superiority against any celebrity I had previously strummed myself off to in recent memory.

He smiled, a rueful grin that may have just burst my heart. I worked my jaw, trying to formulate speech, glancing back and forth from the slippers to his face.

"Would you like these?" His voice. Sandpaper over the hull of a yacht. A combination of roughness and polish.

I swallowed. "The slippers?" Of course the slippers. What else would he be talking about?

A surprised look crossed his face. "You're Southern. From ... Alabama?"

"Florida. Just south of the Georgia border." I winced. I couldn't hide the drawl; it dragged through my words with such ownership, as if the Southern notes were fused through every syllable.

He nodded slowly, still holding out the slippers. His other hand moved, reaching across. "I'm Brett."

I should stand. It would be the polite thing to do. Stand and shake his hand. But I didn't. I didn't think my feet could handle it. I just reached out, shook his hand with a firm grip, like my daddy taught me, and met his eyes. "Riley."

I didn't know what about that exchange he found funny, but his mouth widened, and I got another devastating look at his teeth. God, I'd love for him to nibble my skin. Tease my neck, take the other, more sensitive parts of my body and wreak havoc on them. I shivered at the thought and pulled my eyes from his. Took the slippers from his hands. "You carry around slippers?"

"I saw your hobble across the casino. It caught my eye. I wandered out, wanted to make sure a man didn't take advantage of your ill state."

"By what? Swooping to my rescue with ridiculously comfortable slippers?"

If possible, his grin widened. "Yes. You should probably avoid me from this point forward."

Having no intelligent response, I pretended to distract myself from the conversation, working the soft cotton over my injured feet and sighing with relief when they were on. "Where did you get these?"

He tilted his head to the right. "The store next door. They carry matching robes if you'd like to complete the look."

I laughed. "No, I'm good."

"I would have offered to carry you, but it didn't seem appropriate. When I saw that you had sat down ... How far do you have to go?"

"My room." I waved a hand dismissively in the direction of our room. "Coral Towers."

He frowned. "A bit of a hike."

"It was." I wiggled my toes. "A lot better now. Please sit down." I gestured to the seat next to me. Pulled open my purse and dug through the chips there, saw him, out of my peripheral, remain standing. *Okay.* I collected all of the green chips I could find. Six total. Sixty bucks' worth. I closed my purse and held out the handful, watched Brett eye my closed fist. "Go on, open your hand," I urged.

He did, wincing when I dropped the chips into his palm. He frowned, rolling them over in his palm and holding them back out to me.

"They're for the slippers." I clasped the top flap of my purse, ignoring the insistent press of his fist in my personal space. I batted off his hand. "Take it."

"I don't want your money."

"I don't want your charity. Please."

"It's not charity." Stubbornness entered his voice, and I fought the urge to smile.

"It's giving me something for nothing ... that's charity."

"I've had the pleasure of your company."

I sniffed in a manner that would, most certainly, make my grandmother roll over in her grave. "For five minutes? Please."

"Then let me accompany you the rest of the way to your room. Just to make sure you arrive safely."

I sighed. A big dramatic one—one that gave no hint to the fact that I hadn't got laid in almost two years, hadn't been on a date in almost half that time, and had *never* looked into a face as gorgeous as this man's. "Just to the door?"

His mouth twitched. "Just to the door. Then you will have properly compensated me for the slippers and will be forced to accept your hard-earned chips back."

"They weren't that hard-earned," I grumbled, heaving to my feet, suddenly aware of the height at which my yep-definitely-too-old-to-wear-this minidress had risen. I worked it back down, looking up a moment too early and catching his eyes on my legs. My hands froze, his eyes catching my own. He should have brushed it off, looked away, but instead he held my gaze and grinned, a slow, sexy smile that grabbed ahold of my arousal lever and pushed that baby all the way up. *Damn.* This man and his fuzzy slippers, his bad boy smile and roaring confidence ... I didn't belong anywhere within miles of him. My blistered feet and I were way too vulnerable for the train wreck to which we were headed. Because I knew what would happen when we got through the long walk to my room. All he would have to do is tilt his head, grin that naughty smile, and my ass would tumble over itself in a haste to do anything and everything he wanted.

I reached up and accepted his outstretched hand. He smiled down at me, our heights thrown off by my lack of heels. *Oops, my shoes.* I crouched, scooping up my heels, my eyes suddenly friendly to their sparkling straps, their impossible heights that I was naïve to think I could handle. I gripped his hand and shuffled forward, the soft pat of the slippers quiet on the tile floor.

"Feel free to lean on me," he said, looking down on me with a smile. "And if you need to be carried..."

"I'll be fine." I grinned. "Promise."

He tugged gently, and we moved, through the shops, my hand foreign in another hand, and I released his arm and gripped his bicep instead, marveling at the strength, fighting the urge to squeeze and test the hard muscle.

chapter 2

"Are you here alone?"

I glanced over, our hands separated eight paces back, when the contact had become awkward. "No. There are six of us. Bachelorette party."

I might have been mistaken, but I felt as if he stumbled slightly, a hitch in his step. "Yours?"

The three martinis from dinner made that question much more humorous than it should've been, and I giggled. "*Me*? No."

"A boyfriend?" We arrived in the lobby, and he reached out, placing a firm hand on my arm, making sure I made the journey down the short bank of steps without incident.

I shook my head. "No." I looked over. "Is there a Mrs. Brett?"

He chewed on his bottom lip as he met my eyes, the first bit of indecision that I'd seen on his face. And damn, it was a hot look. He should rock indecision more often. The bite of white teeth combined with a tight jaw, rough stubble paired with intense eyes. "I wouldn't be escorting you if I was attached."

I looked away from his face, breaking the connection before I tackled him to the ground and had my Southern way with him. We reached the elevators and stopped, his finger pressing the button.

Silence. Awkward silence. I shifted in the slippers, trying to look anywhere but in his general direction. I should be better at this. I was thirty-two for God's sake, not a fifteen-year-old girl with her date to the prom. "Are you here on business?"

He grinned, his head shaking, his hand gesturing for me to go ahead when the elevator doors opened. "No. I'm with a few friends. Blowing off some steam."

I pressed the button for the eighth floor, leaning back against the wall, putting as much distance between us as possible. He took my lead, settling against the opposite wall, his stance relaxed, the lines of his dress shirt falling perfectly over dark jeans. I raised my eyebrows, my mouth curving into a smile. "Blowing off some steam?"

Our conversation was interrupted, a hand shooting in and catching the closing doors, the action stalling and then reversing their close. Three men stepped on. Not really men. What appeared to be twenty-year-old boys, the smell of alcohol pressing into the car with them, their glassy eyes and curses preceding their entry. I saw Brett's eyes darken, the space between us suddenly full.

"What floor?" I asked when the doors closed and their attention hadn't moved, no button pressed, the elevator already starting an ascent.

Mistake. Their eyes moved as one, locking on me, and the man closest to me stumbled, moving into my comfort zone. "What floor are *you* going to?" he slurred, the question causing encouraging laughter from his friends, one who cast a quick look in Brett's direction.

"Leave her alone." The tightness in Brett's voice surprised me, and I looked up to his face, caught off guard by the hard line of his jaw, the heat in his stare, his eyes on the men and not on mine. I wanted to reassure him, not that we were friendly enough that I would assume his protection. But it seemed—from the stiffness of his body, his push off the wall and onto the balls of his feet, the iron in his tone—that he was ready to fight, to defend, to do all the unnecessary things that this bevy of boys was not looking for.

The doors slid open, and I squeezed through the men, their steps slow to move, Brett's arm knocking them back, grumbled curses following the action, a cowardly shout of rebellion sent out right as the doors closed. We stood in the empty landing.

"Are you okay?" His eyes were dark, face tight. I glanced down and saw his fists clenched.

I laughed, pressed a light hand on his chest. "I'm fine. They were drunk. It would have been fine."

He gripped my forearms, walked me three steps backward, until I was against the wall, and he was close enough to kiss, his face tilted down to me. "Don't assume that. Never assume that."

Then he closed the gap, his fingers tightening on my arms, squeezing so there was almost pain, his mouth possessive and rough at first contact but melting instantly, his hands loosening, running up my forearms until they reached my shoulders, then past that to cup my face. A sound came from me, something between a sigh and a moan, and he caught it on his tongue, our mouths molding into a fire of hot debate, the fight of our tongues one that turned into a dance of seduction—him pushing, me pulling, the press of his body getting tighter and tighter to mine, until I was on my toes, and the weight of him pressed me against the wall.

In a moment of pause I spoke, my voice gasping, my senses overwhelmed, the only thing I knew was that I wanted him too much to think straight, too much to make a coherent decision right now. "Wait." I placed a hand on his chest, and he immediately dragged his mouth off mine, his eyes fierce, tight to mine, as he took his own ragged breath of air.

"I'm sorry. I'm not used to ... restraint." His hands released their grip on my hair, our connection broken, and I sank to my heels, my mouth raw, my body throbbing ... wanting ... more. *He's not used to restraint?* I wasn't used to touch, to the taste of another's mouth. It'd been years since I'd had a cock in my mouth, years since I'd felt a man's skin beneath my touch, much less his hands on my body. I needed to step away from this man. I needed to get in my room, away from his cocky smile, his eyes that ate my soul, his hands that burned like possessive fire across my skin. I couldn't control myself in his presence, wouldn't be able to keep myself from yanking out his cock, pulling up my dress, and spreading my legs wide open.

He took another step back, rubbed his mouth. "I'm sorry. I shouldn't have done that."

I'm not. I blushed. "It's fine. I didn't exactly stop you." I pushed off the wall, trusting my feet to hold me. I must move away. I wanted him so badly. What was I doing? My new slippers moved me silently forward. Beside me, his hands disappeared inside his pockets, his head cast down. I stopped in front of my room, took a steadying breath, and turned to him. "This is it. Thank you."

His right hand was outstretched, fist closed. I stared at it in confusion before I realized what he was doing. I gave him an exasperated smile and held my hands out together, cupped beneath his fist, the chips falling into my palms with a dull clink. "I *wanted* to pay you for the slippers."

He chewed on his lip again, the move an apparent habit, and stared at me as if sorting out something in his mind. Silence drew out, thickness in the air between us. God, I wanted to suck on that lip. Grab it between my teeth and suck. I fought the urge to squirm, the need between my legs crawling up my stomach and dragging on my breasts with its want.

He finally spoke, breaking our eye contact as he looked away. "I don't want your money. It was my pleasure."

I felt ridiculous, both of my hands closed around the chips. Like I was a Chinese doll ready to bow in respect. He didn't seem pushy about coming in, my fears of wanton sluthood unnecessary given his proximity to my body. I shouldered my purse open and dumped the chips, fishing out my room key, then looked down at my feet. "Want the slippers? You could run back down. Do this whole bit again on a new victim of poor fashion decisions."

"Nah." He leaned one hand against the wall, the action bringing him a foot closer, still a safe distance away. "I'll end the night while I'm up." He pushed off the wall, held out his hand, that gorgeous mouth stretching into a smile. "Nice to meet you, Riley."

"Back 'atcha Brett." I shook his hand, releasing it quickly. Either I was imagining it, and was in serious danger of embarrassing the hell outta myself, or we were one slip away from headboard-banging a hole through to the next room.

I inserted the key, pushed down the handle, and stepped in, giving him a small wave before gently shutting the door. It clicked, and I stared at the white wood. Somewhere, in the region between my legs, my sex drive sobbed in despair. Okay, this was fine. I made it safely to the room, was now alone. *Alone.* No hot hands ripping at my clothes, his mouth hungry on my neck, his cock pressing against my skin before pushing deep and hard where I was in desperate need of it. *Fuck.* Somewhere, my brain bumped around and tried to find the place of reason where my decision to not invite him in was a good one. Surely it was the right move. I had maintained my composure. I did not become *that* girl, the one who allowed horny desire to put her in harm's way. Despite that man's gasp-worthy looks, chivalrous actions, and mypantiesarestillwet kissing ability, I didn't know him. He was a stranger. This was not Quincy, Florida. I did not know his parents, did not grow up sitting next to him on sticky bus seats. I couldn't invite him in. Shouldn't. Probably wouldn't ever. I rose to my tiptoes and looked through the peephole.

He was still there. Staring at the floor, the back of his hand to his mouth. He ran a hand through his hair, slowly, then with rough aggression. Then, he was gone. I looked as far as I could, the peephole giving me a limited view of the world. I wanted to open the door, to peek outside and see him. To see whether he was striding confidently down the hall, or moving hesitantly on to the next part of his night. But I didn't. I dropped my heels by the door, kicked off the slippers, and took four steps, falling onto the closest bed.

chapter 3
Kitten

In college, I owned half a dorm, my roommate a South Floridian princess who chain-smoked Virginia Slims when not having angry, scream-at-each-other sex with her boyfriend. The room was tiny—a 10x10 space divided down the middle by hot pink duct tape. We'd put the tape down on the first day, our parents beaming and shaking hands, each so proud of 'their girl,' the mix of cultures tropical and exciting in the feminine space.

I now lived in a space the same size. I'd walked it off countless times, sometimes the scrape of chain accompanying my steps, other times unencumbered. It was twelve of my feet long, six of my feet wide. On the back side was a windowless concrete wall, painted a lifetime ago some shade of white that was now gray. On the front side, a line of metal pipes held in place by concrete. I'd tried to move them, jiggle them, scrape at their footers. They weren't going anywhere.

My cramped space held a toilet, shower, and bed. He often brought in a chair, but he took it with him when he left. I would tell you how long I'd been here, but I didn't know.

chapter 4

The next morning, I woke up thinking of Brett. The possessive grip of his fingers, the need in his mouth, the press of his body against me, the heat between our touch. The way my body had cried out and his had responded.

Circumstance brought me back to Earth, reminding me, with the cruel pairing of sunlight rays, that he'd left. Had the opportunity to escort me in, get my number, or, at the very least, rock my world with one more kiss. But instead he'd run. Or rather, walked. With a gentleman's goodbye and nothing more.

I took a shower. Pathetic water pressure that alternated between hot and lukewarm. Squeezed out a mini bottle of shampoo with a British crest, yet made in Illinois. I dried off hard enough to realize that my back was sunburnt, the itch and scratch of the towel rough against my tender skin. Wrapping the white terrycloth around my body, I walked to the closet. Stared at my open suitcase, then at the clothes hanging. Nothing looked good enough.

I was too old to feel that way, the adolescent, breathless high. Nervous anticipation at the idea that I might walk downstairs and bump into his gaze. The tingling feeling that I might have met my soul mate, kissed his mouth, gazed up into his face and felt his smile touch my skin. Was I one of hundreds? Just another girl, just a brief experience that he would think nothing of? Did I imagine the spark, the connection? My leg was jiggling, jumping up and down underneath the desk as I applied mascara with a hand that was too shaky. The resort was huge. We were leaving in twenty-eight hours. I'd probably never see him again. I should have gotten his number.

"Shut the curtains, bitch."

I ignored the words, examined my blue sundress, and wondered if the deodorant marks skipping along the front would rub out.

"Seriously. What time is it?"

"Nine-twenty." I tossed the dress down, gave up on looking put-together, and grabbed a pair of shorts and a tank top. That was about as fashion forward as my town got. It would have to be good enough.

"Fuuuccccckk..." The word was muffled under ten pounds of hangover and one mascara-smeared pillow, but it was there. I had about five minutes before Tammy not-a-morning-person McGowan rolled her ass out of bed, and I didn't plan to be in striking distance when that happened.

"Coffee's brewed. We're supposed to be at the spa at ten. I'm gonna run downstairs and grab breakfast."

A grunt. Muffled curses. I grabbed my purse and room key, opened the door, and escaped.

The hotel's prices would make a nun curse like Tammy. I ordered a bottled water, apple, and blueberry muffin from the coffee stand in the lobby and still racked up an eighteen-dollar bill, fifteen percent gratuity automatically added. And for that additional three bucks I didn't even get a smile. I scribbled my last name and room number, signed the line, and snagged my tray of food, elbowing open the door and stepping onto the balcony, picking a table by the railing and settling in.

Wedge sandals kicked off, my chipped pink toes curled against the stone railing, brilliant blue water sparkled at me from behind one hundred acres of palm trees and resort pools. A pigeon missing the toes on his right foot landed on the railing three feet to my right and tilted his head at my feet as if he might give them a taste. I tossed him a piece of muffin, then kicked out my foot, leaning my head back once I was convinced that my still-blistered-from-last-night piggies were safe.

Peeled the sticker from the apple. Crunched. Chewed. Swallowed. The sun was warm, even that early. And no humidity. God, I wished our section of Florida was like this. Heat without the moisture bath that made sweat bead on my upper lip. Here, I could bake for hours. High enough up for a breeze, the sun warming me with a gentle embrace, I took a swig of water and then screwed the lid back on. Loosened the muscles in my neck, slid down a little in my chair, and closed my eyes. Good ol' alone time. Fifteen minutes, maybe twenty. Then I would need to get my ass over to the spa for three hours of feminine chatter. Go Team McCrory.

A breeze blew from behind, ruffling the light hair on my forearm. Men's voices had appeared, talking too loud, the scrape of metal against pavers as they settled into the chairs behind me. The click of a lighter as one of them ruined a perfectly healthy set of lungs.

I kept my eyes closed, taking a bite of muffin as my mind wandered, my eavesdropping gene lifting its head when a voice started that sounded familiar. I began to sit up but stopped, not sure if now, sans make-up with a face full of muffin crumbs, was how I wanted to reintroduce myself. I stayed in place, slouching a little further, more certain with each additional word, that one of the men was Brett. A smile played on the corner of my mouth.

"What happened with that girl from last night?"

"The blonde?"

"Yeah. Looked like you were headed up to her room."

A pause. Soft cough. I almost fell off my chair in an attempt to hear his next words.

"Nothing happened. She's here with a bachelorette party. You know how I feel about that."

I didn't pay attention to the other man's response, my toes curling against the railing, body tightening in hurt and anger. *Not his type.* Maybe that was why he walked away so easily. And here I was, thinking the kiss had affected him as deeply as it had me. I dug my nails into my thighs, watching a curl of forgotten smoke float past, hearing the eventual screech of chair legs as the men behind me moved along.

Fuck him. I didn't need a one-night stand anyway. My dusty vagina was perfectly happy with the extensive network of cobwebs it'd spent years creating. Somewhere, in the empty recesses of my mind, my subconscious tore to pieces the 'I love Brett' poster and moved on to more official business.

chapter 5

tight (tīt)
(adj.) closely or densely packed together
"the tight crowd"

Midnight. Thirteen hours left in paradise, then our hung-over selves would be strapped in and flying back to Quincy. I hung an arm around twin necks, inhaling the scent of hairspray and feminine energy, leaned my head back, weight on their shoulders, and bellowed the chorus of "Sweet Home Alabama." The club sang along, and my mouth broke into a grin too big to contain—the familiar tune never failed to raise my spirits. Never mind that, between the six of us, we'd set foot on Alabama soil less than ten times. It was the anthem of the South, and seeing as it took Jena flashing the Bahamian DJ her breasts to get it played, we owned every syllable of the damn thing.

The last chorus rang out, and I released the girls, spinning on the floor, my arms up, getting bumped by sweaty bodies, the dance floor getting tighter by the moment. A heavy bass began, drowning out the country chorus and starting back into the hip-hop that had been dominating the speakers all night.

I slowed my hips, glanced at our table, saw Beth and Tammy there, the rest of us sprinkled between the dance floor and the ladies room. I was pushed forward, hands settling on my waist as a stranger tried to pull me into his crotch-thrusting imitation of a dance. I yanked at his wrists, shooting an annoyed look over my shoulder, and moved to our table, snagging my purse off its surface and moving toward the neon-lit exit sign. Air. I needed air. Air and a moment to regroup, focus. Come to terms with the fact that none of the men in this club would be taking care of my needs tonight. None of them seemed worthy of even a drink. Too young. Too immature. Too available. Too ... not who I was looking for.

I banged through the exit door, the rush of cool night kissing my skin. I took two steps to the right and leaned against the brick exterior wall, legs out, head flat against red brick. God yes. I almost wished I still smoked. I remembered the escapes from life that it provided, the moment to take a pause from the world and do nothing but relax. Now, I didn't need the nicotine—just the combination of air and quiet were enough to ease my tension and take me one step closer to forgetting last night.

I sensed the presence before I saw it. In the shadows to my right. I stiffened, lowering my chin and staring, confronting whoever it was with my gaze. Then he spoke, and I relaxed, need and heat and want flooding my body with just the scrape of my name. In that one word, that one growl, every lie I'd told myself was exposed. I needed him. My body needed him. Wanted more. I had behaved in the hallway of the 8th floor. I had made a mistake. I didn't intend to make another.

"Come here." I tilted my head when I spoke.

He stalked forward, in a suit, his hands leaving his pockets as he walked, his head level, stare direct, and ate me with his eyes as he moved without hesitation, not pausing until he was suddenly against me, his hand firm, gripping the side of my face, his mouth taking mine in a possessive kiss that had me back against the wall, his palm against my skin almost hurting me in its need. I gasped for breath when I could grab it, his kiss desperate, dipping, pulling me tighter. I loved it.

"I need you," he grunted, his free hand sliding up my thigh, pushing my dress inappropriately high, his fingers gripping, squeezing, the heat of his palm sliding over my skin like he owned it, his large hand ending on my ass, and he felt every inch of it as if he was memorizing, worshipping, taking it in his mind as his own.

I need you. "Yes," I gasped, lifting my leg and hooking it around him, the shift in my body opening the place between my legs, his fingers finding and running reverently over the line of silk that kept me tied to the edge of sanity.

The door next to me opened, shielding us for a moment, and I froze behind it, my body tensing. His hand dropped from my face, wrapping around my body, the other hand returning to my ass. Both of them worked in concert and lifted, carrying me into the dark shadows where he had just stood, a new wall replacing the brick, this one rough stucco, and I felt lines of it dig into my sunburned skin as he set me down, his mouth taking a break from the kiss and moving to my neck, the rough journey letting me know the level of his need.

Further proof was against me, his pelvis pressed tighter than possible against my own, the hard ridge of it against my pussy making my breath hitch with every twitch of him along me. God, I wanted this man. Was made weak from his touch yet had never felt this aggressive.

Feather soft brushes against silk. Teasing. Torturing. His hand kept my leg in place, though there was no way I was moving it. Not when it opened me up to him. Not when it kept his iron arousal against the place where I wanted it most. My panties were so wet it was embarrassing. I panted against the night air, struggling for silence, the murmurs of the couple who had stepped outside breaking the silence of the night, the orange embers of their smokes reminding me of their presence, their attention on each other, a giggle escaping from their conversation and sending a moment of intelligent thought to my head. Was I really being humped in the shadows against the side of a building? Was this beautiful man really running the pad of his fingers back and forth, lower and higher, finding the—oh my god. My head dropped back, and I couldn't stop the moan that escaped when his fingers brushed my silk-covered clit.

Jesus. It wasn't a curse. It was a thankful message sent upward. I had been lost, and now, in that light brush against my most sensitive place, I was found.

He chuckled against my neck, his fingers moving back an inch or two, until they were back at my soaked opening, pushing on the indent there, the silk moving far enough inside for me to feel the brush of skin on skin, and I just about lifted off the ground in my need for more.

"Don't stop," I gasped.

"Honey, I'm not going to stop until you fall apart in my hands. I need that. I'm not releasing you until it happens."

He lifted his mouth off my neck, returning to my mouth, his kisses softening as his fingers took their time, probing, fluttering over my clit, sliding a firm index down the line, making their way to my ass for a hard press, before returning and starting the insanity again. I was shaking, wanting, *dying* for another touch of his skin, wanting the silk tease of my panties gone, wanting the raw feel of skin on skin. Even with that need, I was not prepared when it happened, my mouth freezing against his kiss, brain function gone, motor skills impaired, every intelligent thought I ever had fleeing my body as his thumb pressed against my clit and two of his fingers pushed inside my body.

Holy Jesus Hell.

He groaned, his forehead on my own, pushing my head back against the wall. "Fuck, I wish you were open before me on a bed right now so I could see this." The words tore from him, and through the blurred vision of my senses I saw the couple glance our way, a whispered discussion beginning, then ending; the club door opened.

"If we were on a bed right now, your cock would be out." It was a difficult sentence to formulate, my hips thrusting, trying to help the push and withdrawal of his fingers, my eyes closing despite my best attempts to keep them open.

"Is that so?"

I could hear his need despite the cocky drawl of his question. I had my leg wrapped around him, could feel a tremor in his legs, could feel the stiff ridge of his cock that was anything but unaffected.

"I'm—" The word 'close' never made it off my lips. It couldn't, never had a chance at life, my orgasm eating it for dessert with a ravenous need that took hold of everything else in its path. I tightened around his fingers, my body shuddering as delirium moved in needy waves, radiating from the center of my universe, which laid in the slick breath between his fingers and my everything. I didn't catch the first of his words; they disappeared in my full body experience. But then later, I heard them as I fell back down to Earth, the vowels stretching out my grip on insanity, taking me to an additional plane I had never reached before.

"... beautiful creature. You feel so perfect. So open, so willing. I want to take every piece of you. Open up your world. Taste you on my mouth. Feel this sensation against the bare skin of my cock. God, I want you so badly. Have thought about you all day."

His mouth stopped moving, stopped talking, crushed back on mine, communicating the most with its desperation, his fingers thrusting and then slowly halting their movement, and just stayed in place, buried inside, my body fuller than it had been in a long time. I dropped my hand off his shoulders, let the one that had been digging lines of need into his back fall as a wave of sexual contentment moved in.

His mouth slowed, and he slid my leg down, tugged my dress back, keeping our kiss uninterrupted, his hands moving to cup both sides of my face as his legs straddled mine, my push against the wall less intense as our interaction changed to something less dirty. He broke the kiss, resting his forehead against my own as he let out a long breath that was half groan in its makeup. "God, Riley."

He sounded so pained, so remorseful, that I almost checked for a wedding ring, almost pushed against his chest to look into his eyes. But I didn't. I didn't do anything but enjoy the scent of his cologne, the view out of the bottom of my lashes, one of expensive fabric and a peek of tan skin.

"I don't know what to do with you." He finished the statement with a brush over my lips, his hands lifting my face until it was turned up to him, our eyes meeting for the first moment since I lost all sense.

Damn, I could look in this man's eyes all day. Could get lost in them, move for them, lie, steal, die for them. I stared in his eyes and fully accepted that I was a woman. Vulnerable, emotional, delicate, easily overcome. I didn't know this man. Had shared less than a hundred sentences with him. Had just given him a piece of my virtue in the form of a finger fuck on a dirty Bahamian street in the dead of night.

I stared in his eyes and said nothing. Memorized the dark depths of them. The thick fringe of lashes that I'd accuse of being mascara-enhanced had he not radiated masculinity from every pore on his body.

"I don't need to ask if you do this often. Your body betrays you of the impossibility of that fact." He spoke tightly, his hands keeping my face up, my eyes arrested by him, not that I had any plans of looking away in this lifetime. "I don't. I can't. This ... is not normal." His eyes dropped to my lips and he bent, took a long draw of my mouth, as if it was the last time we would ever kiss. He groaned, and my shoulders were suddenly pushed back against stucco. "Fuck," he swore. "God, I need you underneath me." He released me, stepped away, rubbed his mouth as he turned, half in the light, the shadows protecting me from the meat of his stare.

"So take me." The voice that came out of me was not my own. It was of a confident woman who admitted what she wanted, took what she needed.

He dropped his hand, stared at me. "You don't mean that. You'd regret it in the morning. And I don't do one-night stands."

"Meaning?" I stayed against the wall. He could come to me if he wanted something. I didn't know if, at this point, my legs had the capacity to move anyway.

He did come. Was in front of me in three strides, his hands on either side of my head, flat against the wall, his eyes intense, inches from mine. I smelled the faint scent of whiskey on his breath. I noticed the angle of his body, his hips too far away when all I wanted was them pressed against me. Was he still hard? 'Cause I was still wet. Desperately so. "Meaning," he growled, "that if I have you, you will not return to life as you know it. You will not flirt with men around the water cooler at work. You will bend for me, spread for me, allow me to have every inch of your surface, all while screaming my name and shuddering into my heart. That is what I mean."

Holy shit. I tried to breathe normally. Tried to stop my pulse from jumping through my skin. Tried to speak in a way that didn't cause my voice to shake. "We don't have water coolers."

He smiled, and the change pulled me off whatever ledge I gripped. Oh my word. White, perfect teeth. A goddamn mischievous twinkle in his eyes. I couldn't figure out if I liked his intense side or smiling side more, but I tried and held on to this look for as long as I could. "And the rest?"

"I don't think that's a decision I can make without having your cock first."

He tilted his head. "Worried I will disappoint?"

Hell to the no. "Girl's gotta be safe." I released my own smile, one with much less potency, but the best card I had in this situation.

His face darkened, the grin disappearing as intensity stole back over. "I'm not joking, Riley. About having you."

I watched his eyes, the shudder in them as they looked from my lips to my eyes to the door. All minute twitches of his pupils, his head unmoving, his entire body so still it could have been made of steel. Controlled intensity. I didn't doubt his words. I also knew that there was no way I could say anything but yes to this man. My body wouldn't allow any other response. "Then take me."

Confirmation in the set of his face, the fire that came to his eyes, the forward press of his pelvis as he gathered me back, pulling me tightly, his mouth coming back down to claim me. Yes, he was still hard. I smiled against his mouth.

chapter 6
Kitten

tight (tīt)
(adj.) strictly imposed
"he kept tight control"

For a small period of time, I was able to keep track of my days. On the wall below my bed, in the dark space hidden by sheets and shadows, I scratched lines in plaster. One line every night. I marked them slowly, the scrape of the butter knife's edge wearing smooth, the repeated action breaking through the grime, my movements patient, the act ritualistic.

He discovered the marks on the twelfth day, his reaction a mixed bag of delight and intrigue. He crouched, looked at the marks in the same way a parent would look at a school project. I watched from the corner, my arms cuffed to the front bars, butt on the floor, as he stripped my bed. My exertions during training had moved it slightly, and, when he bent to push it back, he paused, his eyes catching my lines, his haste to pull the bed back almost comical in its excitement.

"You did this?" he asked, glancing over his shoulder at me. I said nothing, watching as his fingers scrolled lightly over my hard work. "Eleven." He repeated the number, his head tilting at something that came to mind, and he leaped up, grabbing his notepad and frantically flipped pages. "Eleven." He looked up at me. "Eleven days ago I took off your handcuffs. Gave you freedom in the room." He glanced around. "How did you know what a day was? There aren't any windows in this room. And the lights are always on." His eyebrows pinched.

I swallowed. "You visit every day. Wear different clothes. That's how I count." He stared at me for a spell before pulling a pen from the notebook and writing, a long line of cursive that wasn't legible from my seat on the floor. I took a risk. "How long did it take for you to take off my handcuffs? To give me that freedom?"

He laughed, jotting down something in the margin before clicking the pen shut. "Great question, Kitten. But I can't tell you that. And I can't let you do this. Counting days signifies hope. We can't have hope."

"Why not? Wouldn't hope endear me to you?"

He walked over, crouched before me. I dropped my eyes, examining the seam of his dress pants as they stretched over his knee. "No Kitten," he whispered. "Believe me when I say that hope will only drive you insane."

That night, when he left, he chained me back up. I didn't know how long, how many days stretched by while I was back in those cuffs, but when he let me free, I didn't keep any more hatch marks. I couldn't. He varied his schedule, visited a bunch in a row, then would leave me for what felt like days. I cursed myself for speaking, swore - for at least a week - to not tell him anything. I didn't keep that vow. A part of me felt that the only thing he wanted me for was information. And once he had all of that, maybe he'd let me go.

Or, maybe he'd kill me.

I had to face all options.

chapter 7

The driver's name was Leo. White Escalade with custom rims, tinted windows. I stepped into the backseat, Brett following me inside, his long legs cramped in the backseat. I clutched my purse, smiled at Leo as he shut the door. I had parted with the girls, their protective nature insisting on a face to face with Brett before letting me disappear into the night. Jena had taken it one step further, getting his business card and verifying his cell. He smiled through it all, relaxed and at ease, the intensity of our alley romp gone as he shook hands, *oh my god, those fingers were in me*, remembered names, and stole all of their hearts.

The SUV moved, rocking over cobblestone steps that pirates once roamed, the movement of the car tossing me slightly. Brett's hand found me in the darkness.

"Sorry about the interrogation in there."

"I'm not. They're watching out for you. It's the smart thing to do."

I bit the edge of my smile. "You say that. Jena Crawford has your number. You might regret that in the wee hours of the morning. I think her second major was drunk dialing."

He brought my hand to his mouth, kissing the back of it. "I can handle it."

I glanced to the front. To the Bahamian man less than five feet away. "What you said in the alley, about what this will mean..."

"Yes."

I shrugged. "I just want you to know that I'm a big girl. I'm not gonna attach anything to this. If it doesn't turn out to be anything."

He looked out the window. Tugged at the front of his dress pants, adjusting himself, he said, "I may have spoken out of turn. I'm not used to this."

I lowered my voice. "We can have sex. Without it meaning anything."

"I'm not seventeen, Riley. I'm familiar with the concept."

I shut my mouth. Did my own turn of looking out the window, trying to decide if I should bail on this man when we hit the hotel lobby. It was easier when I looked out the window. When I didn't see the line of his jaw and imagine how it tasted. When I didn't look in those eyes and fall further into trouble. He moved my hand, from the armrest where he had held it, to his lap. I pushed my palm flat against him, and lost a bit of my breath. Wow.

His hand atop mine, he slid my palm—my exploring, inquisitive fingers—from his belt buckle to his leg, letting me feel exactly how much, how hard, he wanted me. I darted my eyes, tried to see more, but the dark cab showed me nothing but the glow of his eyes. Watching me, his mouth hidden by shadow. Those eyes closed briefly when I gripped him through the fabric. "More," he breathed.

I fumbled with the zipper, my own hand struggling, his hand moving to help, holding the fabric tightly as I tugged down the metal tag, holding my breath, hoping the driver's music would drown out the sound, the man's head not moving, not turning. When the action ended, my hand stole in and came in immediate contact with bare cock.

There was a moment when my body relaxed as my fingers wrapped around it, as if I was finally at peace in a place where I belonged and everything else could subside. *I am touching it.* The thought was a shot of arousal to my body. I moved my hand, explored. My first thought, the observation that my thumb and index finger didn't meet. That his fingers, which had satisfied me so easily in that alley, wouldn't hold a candle to this organ. I squirmed a bit in my seat. Gripped him with my full hand and was rewarded with an exhale of breath.

A squeal of brakes. I looked up and realized we were stopping. It was a tollbooth, Leo leaning out the window, the street lights of the toll plaza casting in full light, my hand on Brett's *ohmygodthatisgorgeous* cock. He leaned forward quickly, pushing my hand gently to the side, and my ears heard the faint sound of a zipper closing.

"Royal Towers." He put his hands on the front headrests, resting his weight on them as he spoke to the driver, and I fought the urge to run my hand over the line of his back. It'd been so long since I touched a man in a loving way. So long since I was in a role other than that of professional friend—sweet ol' Riley.

I didn't touch his back. I sat, my hands between my knees, the heat of my fingers remembering the lines of his cock. The ridge between his shaft and his head. How it moved slightly in my hand when I grabbed it. The warmth of his skin.

Then the truck stopped, a burst of air brushed over my bare legs, and I accepted Leo's hand and exited the vehicle.

"Thank you." Brett's hand was on my arm, taking over from Leo, firm pressure in his touch as he guided me toward the entrance, his steps quick, my heels almost struggling to keep up. I tugged on his hand, and his head turned, noted my agitation, and he slowed his gait. "I'm sorry." He looped an arm around my shoulders, pressed a kiss on the top of my head. "Do you want to grab a drink at the bar?"

Do I want to grab a drink at the bar? I didn't think I could handle the wait to walk down the hotel hallway, much less sit out the agonizing process of ordering, sipping, and then paying for an unneeded drink. I shook my head. "No. I'm good."

He held the door, our eyes catching for a moment as I passed through. Just that catch, that brief hold of two stares ... it relit the fire that didn't need any additional fuel. I didn't know why I was going to fuck this man. There was no sense or reason in the decision. But there was need. There was need, and there would be satisfaction. I didn't know what was about to happen, but I knew it would be different than anything I had ever had. Anyone I had ever fucked. I felt like I did when I was a virgin. Nervous. Apprehensive. Excited. The hand on my back guided me to an unfamiliar elevator, and I waited as he pressed the button.

CHAPTER 8
BRETT

I watched her. *This is a mistake*. I should be back in that alley. Or in the smoke of the club. Drinking. Watching. Doing what I came to do. I wasn't here for entertainment, didn't court strange women into my bed. My head, my heart, didn't understand that. Fucking should have a purpose, should contribute to an end goal. There was no end goal that would work in this scenario. She was practically from *Georgia* for God's sake. Here on a bachelorette party, surrounded by a group of friends with eyes of hawks and sex drives of donkeys. A fuck with her would accomplish nothing, lead nowhere. The words my idiotic mouth had uttered in that alley would never work. What did I expect? That after a few hours in my bed, she would commit? Fill the hole that once held my heart? This woman who moved before me, the one who smelled of lilies and brown sugar, had her own life. One I knew nothing about. A life that breathed fire and independence. One with roots and commitments and, for all I knew, its own leading man. I watched as the elevator doors opened and she stepped out, my hand reaching, snagging the delicate warmth of her wrist, and dragging her to the side, rougher than necessary, my sudden need to know more asserting its dominance. I released her wrist when she stumbled sideways, catching her weight and pinning it against the closest wall.

"Jeez." The word came out as an annoyed huff, her eyes flashing as I moved closer, placed a hand on the wall beside her head, and stared into her eyes. "What is it with you and walls?"

"What's it about you?"

"Me?" She lifted her chin, looked at me head on.

"I can't stop myself. I want to pin you and fuck you against every surface I come to." I swallowed. Refocused my agitation on reading her signs.

Her body tightened. Breath shortened. Eyes focused on my mouth. All reactions I was familiar with. Could read as easily as a financial statement. *Lust.* A struggle against the reaction, her mind arguing with her want, her eyes losing focus as she licked her lips to wet them. *Good God.* I barely heard her moan, heard the sound sigh out of her lips as she leaned against the wall, and I let myself do what I'd thought about for the last fifteen minutes. Tasted that sweet fucking tongue. Reached down and lifted her up. Wrapped her legs around my waist and carried her the short distance to the door, my hand fumbling with the key, our mouths fighting in their frantic quest for moremoremore. I turned the handle, pushed the door, stepped into the darkness and carried her to the bed. Tossing her off, I took a moment to catch my breath. Collect my wits. From behind, I heard the click of the closing door and, for the first time since meeting, we were truly and completely alone together. I sent a short prayer upward for strength, restraint, the ability to touch her and be gentle.

chapter 9

"Stay here." His breath seemed harder than necessary, the wild look in his eyes enough to keep me in place, my own lust aiding in the desire to speed this process along. He stepped away, running a hand through his hair, moved to the doors at the end of the room, opened the slider fully. Standing there for a moment, his hands high on the doorframe, his head hung slightly as he appeared to think.

I propped myself up. Made a conscious decision to ignore his directive and stood. Walked across the room until I was behind him. His back straightened, and he turned, his face dark, silhouetted by the lit night before him.

I stopped. Looked up into the darkness that was his face. His hand reached forward, toward my face, and I flinched, his hand stopping a few inches away.

"Relax." His hand moved slowly, brushing down and covering my eyes. "Close your eyes."

I did. I closed my eyes and felt his hand drop. Kept them closed as I turned every other sense to high alert. "Good girl," he said softly. "Keep them closed."

I did. I kept my world dark and tried to relax. Felt the heat of him as he moved closer. I inhaled, but only smelled ocean, the breeze from the open door washing the scent of salt and sea across my face. Then his hands brushed over my shoulder blades, tugging down the spaghetti straps of my dress. Swiped back across my collarbone as his firm fingers tugged at the front clasp of my dress. There was absolute silence as he parted the fabric and slid it down until my bra was the only thing on my upper half.

Closer. I could feel the brush of his chest against the soft pillow of my breasts. Both of his arms wrapped around me as he unclipped my bra in one movement, the garment dropping, my breasts suddenly loose and free. His arms fell and the hard comfort of his body left me. My eyes flipped open.

"No." He was before me. Staring. Close enough that the shadow was lifted; I could see the reflection of the bathroom light in his eyes. They were tight on me, a warning look in them. "Keep them closed, Riley. For now."

For now. I released a slow breath. Dropped my eyelids until I was back to relying on touch, smell, hearing. I didn't know why I opened them anyway. This way was so much better. I could let my imagination go wild. Imagine what I wanted. Enjoy what I—oh God. A breeze blew, the cool air causing my skin to awaken, the caress of the outdoors making this suddenly so erotic in its voyeurism. I didn't remember which floor we were on. Didn't know if it's the second or twentieth, but knowing that the balcony door was open before me, feeling the soft brush of his fingers as they returned to my skin ... it was enough to make my nipples peak, the weight in my pussy heavy with its increased need.

"You are so beautiful." He almost groaned the words, the sentence cutting off my own gasp as both of his fingers circled and squeezed my breasts. Lifted them. I felt the rough prickle of his cheek as his mouth moved across their surface. A wet suction as my right nipple made its way into his mouth, his soft play of tongue against delicate skin probing and teasing, a low moan coming out of me when he bit the tip gently. I sagged a bit in his hands, my knees shaking, my desire to have him making a persuasive argument against the one to have him never stop what was occurring right then. "Wait, Riley." His mouth moved lower, his hands released my breasts, and I felt the bump of cloth against my legs.

His mouth pressed kisses along my stomach until it reached the line of my dress, and his hands were suddenly at the back of me, fumbling over and then finding the zipper, yanking it down in one movement, and the fabric fell, leaving me one wet pair of panties away from being naked in heels before him.

"God." A reverent whisper from his mouth. A mouth that was wasting no time in moving lower. "Spread your legs a bit."

I obeyed. Moaned softly when I felt the press of his finger moving aside the silk and pushing inside of me. One gentle push inside that broke any chance of restraint I had left. I opened my eyes, looked down to find him on his knees, and reached out, gripped his hair, and pulled his head back until our eyes met. "I can't," I gasped, his finger pushing deeper, hooking inside of me, his eyes watching me darkly, the edge of his mouth curving a little when my legs buckled.

Thank God the man listened. He moved to his feet, pulling his finger from me and moving it to his mouth. Sucking on his forefinger, he stared down at me. I stepped forward, pulled his finger from his lips and replaced it with my tongue, the man taking my mouth as if he owned it, his hands gripping me to him, his kiss hard and dominant.

I fell back on the bed, his body above me, knees moving to either side of me as he took a final pull on my mouth before sitting up, skimming his fingers down my breasts, the lines of my stomach, hooking into the sides of my panties and dragging them over my hips, his body rolling off me enough to free my body from the last bit of resistance.

"My turn," I breathed, sitting up and reaching for his belt. He obliged, rolling onto his back and letting me unbutton his shirt.

I am nervous. I realized it as my fingers looped buttons through holes, each minor accomplishment revealing inch after inch of strong chest, covered by a thin layer of hair. He was a man, more man than anyone I had been with. My last boyfriend was a leftover from college, a frat boy turned pharmacist, who never let go of the shaggy haircut that every boy from the South seems to don like a badge of honor. This man, whose chest was strong and wide, his eyes dark and heated, his touch, which trailed patiently down my back, was firm and confident.

I pulled at his shirt, tugging fabric from pants until abs were fully exposed, a line of thicker hair leading down the ripped path of his stomach to a belt buckle, a break of skin against dark fabric. I slowed down, pulled hesitantly on the leather, the cold metal of the clasp so foreign in this hot bed of sexual tension. Then his hands pushed me aside, three quick movements having his pants undone, zipper down, belt open, and cock out.

The groan out of me was unstoppable. It rumbled, turned into a hiss, and then my hesitation was gone, and I pounced on it, diving with greedy lips, my frantic fingers trying to pull him down the bed, as I slid down his body and onto my knees on the carpet. I needed it all. I needed to feel the slide of skin against stiff, needed to feel it respond on my tongue. I wanted to taste every inch of it. Suck on his head until he gasped. Take him as far down my throat as I could, damn the gag reflex. Obsessively worship him with my mouth until he was half as hungry with lust as I was.

I couldn't believe I was doing this. On my knees, in a stranger's hotel room, his body following my lead, sliding to the end of the bed, sitting up, his hand settling on the back of my head, pushing with encouragement as I took his gorgeous cock in my mouth. I was naked in front of this man, any prior relationship with modesty having jumped ship, his eyes nothing but worshipping in their perusal of my curves.

He was almost without taste and my mouth worked hard, yearning for a response, the squeeze of sweet hitting my tongue. And, despite my subservient position on my knees, it was empowering to have his most sensitive organ in my mouth. I looked up at him, my eyes watering slightly as he took the moment to pull me further onto his cock. God, the look in his eyes. Singular focus on me. His mouth opened slightly as I increased the pressure of my suction. The ownership of his stare even as his lids dropped slightly, my name came out as a hiss on his lips.

"Get up," he growled. "I need to be inside of you *now*."

His hands were suddenly on my wrists, stopping my motion on his cock. Lifting me to my feet, I was on the bed before I could think, my back dragging across the duvet as he put me into place.

A slowing of time. His hands firm and patient as they spread my legs, opened me before him. Any concern I had over my naked body, the pounds I really should have shed before hitting vacation mode in a bikini ... everything was wiped away by the shudder in his sigh, the look in his eyes as he drank me in, his fingers opening me up, his mouth lowering for a few back-arching seconds as his tongue dipped inside of me.

Then he withdrew. Dragged his fingers down my legs and stopped at my ankle. Worked the strap with his fingers, caressed the curves of my foot as he pulled off the stiletto.

"Is this what you want?"

"My shoes to be taken off?"

The heel dropped to the floor with a soft thud. I looked down, past the V of my legs, at the naked man before me, a hand settling on the outward jut of his cock, wrapping around its base, stroking it as he stared at me, met my eyes, for one silent moment. Salty air swept over my skin, my legs still spread, fingers of coolness softly brushing over my open slit. I was so wet I could feel a drop sliding down the crack of my ass.

"This. What I'm about to do. Is it what you want?"

"Yes." I didn't need to hesitate before speaking the words. I didn't need to think, to analyze. I threw reason and safety and good decisions out the window as soon as I walked through the door to this suite. I traded logic for a touch that I desperately craved, a connection that was dropping that perfect cock and moving to my other foot. Working the straps to that heel. Fingers teasing the arch and ankle there.

The heel came off in his hand, and he tossed it away. Gripped my ankle, moved his knees on the bed, until he was before me, his cock placed against the wet mound. His hands on my inner thighs, delicate movements that were turning rougher, stronger. He pressed on the back of my knees, lifted my legs until my thighs brushed my stomach, shoved forward with his hips, and dragged his hardness back and forth over my clit.

I whimpered. I couldn't help myself. I could feel the loss of control, feel the breakdown of my mind as pleasure took over and I became a loose mess of want before him. I was so close to begging, needed his cock an inch lower so badly I was two steps away from taking that matter into my own hands. "Please." The word slipped from my lips as he continued, the underside of his cock now slick with my juices, the steady drag on my clit so perfect that my plea was suddenly counterproductive seeing as the only thing I wanted to do right then was stay in the moment until I broke.

Shove, pull. Shove, pull. I propped myself up to get a better look, the eroticism of seeing his bare cock, head and shaft tight to the point of ripping, the muscles in his stomach sliding under the tan skin, the evidence of my arousal, my need growing. His skin in the moonlight, reflections of white in his eyes, the groan from his mouth that told me his self-control was as stretched as my own.

I didn't want to come like this. From just the rub of his cock. How tightly stretched was my arousal that just this brush with him could bring me to my knees? I pushed against his chest, squirmed underneath him. "Please, I can't. I'm about to..."

"I need it." His gruff voice was close to my ear. The consistent firm strokes continued, the pump of his cock back and forth, back and ... OH MY.

I stopped it somehow. Gasped for breath. Tried to focus. Tried to fight a battle I was seconds from losing. I didn't know why I was fighting it. How I was managing. All I knew was that every second was incredible, and I didn't want to lose it—couldn't lose it. Not right now. Not just yet. I needed another ten seconds, or fifty, or five hundred. I needed this man to never stop anything he was doing, to—

My elbows gave out and I collapsed, my back bucking, every muscle in my legs contracting as the purest form of ecstasy blinded my world, gripped my heart, and shuddered through my body.

***

A metallic scrape. The rip, crackle. I saw a bit of gold flutter to the scrunched fabric of the white duvet. Moving my eyes to between my legs, I saw the hot brand of his cock lift, busy in his hands, wrapped and secured, then his hands stilled, and I pulled my eyes up, over his stomach, which moved slightly with heavy breaths. Up over the strength of his chest, the defined muscles in his shoulders, the shadow on his face, the swollen curve of his lips. His eyes, blazing with intensity, watched me carefully as he growled out a sigh. I didn't move, didn't pull my eyes from him, but felt the weight of latexed cock against my sensitive clit as he leaned forward slightly, a finger surprising me when he pressed it through the seal of my pussy.

A moan sighed through my lips at the change in his eyes that occurred, the drug of arousal moving through them, dulling his spark, his mouth opening further. He closed his eyes for a moment, his finger moving slowly and deliciously inside of me, and then reopened, control reestablished. I didn't want his control. I wanted him ravaging me, taking me harder, rougher, his strength untapped, sexuality grabbing hold and dragging him by his lapels to the throne of me, where he would forever be my sexual slave.

"Are you sure?"

I groaned in response, his finger cupping, stroking. My core so wet I was shaking for him.

"Answer me. I need to hear it." His voice was rough. Control shaken. *Good.*

I opened my eyes and reestablished contact. Let him see the resolution there. "Yes. Please. Now."

He leaned forward, braced himself above me on the bed, his face a foot from mine, my vision filled with the beautiful look of Brett, and shifted his hips down slightly and thrust.

Mother of—I whimpered, reached up and gripped his shoulders, pulled him closer as my mouth opened in silent exclamation. It had been too long. I couldn't go without it for that long ever again. On second thought, maybe the reason this felt so incredible was because I had been without. But either way, the stretch of my muscles around his cock ... the heat inside me as he slowly thrust, in and out, back and forth, my silent cries turning a little louder, becoming words, moans, begs, pleas. "Don't ever stop ... Brett—I..."

He gave it to me slow. Let me adjust before his speed picked up, thrusts roughening right at the moment when I was ready for it. I wrapped my legs around his waist. Dug my heels into the lickable meat of his ass. Squeezed the heat of his skin with my legs, stared up into his face as he buried his cock in repeated succession, the quickened pace containing an edge of desperation, of wild inhibition.

"Right there, I'm about to..."

I bellowed, the howl of a woman overtaken, and he groaned at the sound, lowered his face to my neck, inhaled my scent as my voice broke. I lost all focus, all ability to understand anything but that he hadn't stopped, hadn't slowed, was carrying me on this high which would not stop until it took hold of my soul and made me his own.

He pulled me back to life, gripped my face with both hands, lowering his face to mine, and dove into my mouth. Kissed me strong. Ragged breaths between deep kisses, his cock continued its steady thrust, my hands greedy against his chest, scraping across the ridges of his side, scratching lines of need into his back. Then he broke the kiss, his hands tightening a little on my face, our eyes holding until a groan dragged from his throat, his eyes closing, head dropping, thrusts slowing and deepening, until he was buried and still inside of me. His hands dropped my face, my name rolled off his lips as he eased down, his body flush to mine, and it felt, in that moment, like we were fused—souls, bodies, and mind—completely together.

chapter 10

My cell was ringing. I heard the familiar tune, the beats dragging me awake, my hand fumbling over the empty bedside table. I woke more, hanging half off the bed as my fingers tripped over carpet until they encountered my purse. I answered it a second short of too late. "Hello?"

"You slut!" The screech of Tammy's voice was way too loud, and I pulled the phone away from my ear. Blinked in the darkness. Tried to figure out where I was. One bed, not two. Room twice as big as the one I spent the prior night in. Movement came from behind me, and I looked over my shoulder to see well over six feet of dark gorgeousness watching me, on his side, the dawn light contrasting with the intense look that he rocked so well. 'Good morning,' he mouthed, his hand reaching out, wrapping around my waist and pulling me flat on my back. He stayed on one side, head propped up on one hand, eyes on my face.

"What do you want?" I mumbled into the phone.

"I just got back to the room. I know your prude ass can't be shacking up with that delicious piece of man you left with last night."

"I can't talk right now."

"You know wheels are going up in three hours."

"Then you should get some more beauty rest."

A snort. The beginning of some lecture. I hung up the phone, locked it and tossed it onto the floor in the direction of my purse, before rolling toward Brett and closing my eyes. I tried to memorize the look of him in morning shadows. It's a good look. Way too good of a look. "I've got to go back to my room."

"No you don't." He bent over, pressing a kiss on my collarbone. Pulled at the sheet, and revealed a breast. He exhaled, moved his mouth to that spot with soft kisses until I pushed him off. Cuddled into the crook of his shoulder. Rested my head on him when he laid back against the pillows.

"I have to go back home."

"When?" The word vibrated through his chest, and I rolled closer into him. Ran my hand over his chest.

"One. Which means I need to pack, and shower..."

"...and eat breakfast."

I looked up. "Maybe."

"I've been told that I'm excellent at ordering room service."

"I've been told that I'm excellent at eating it."

***

We ate on the bed like kids, cross-legged, cartoons on the TV, trays on the crumpled sheets before us. I leaned over, swigged a generous swallow of mimosa from the flute and then returned it to the bedside table. "So ... Mister..." I tilted my head at him. "I don't know your last name."

He scowled. Brought a forkful of omelet to his mouth and chewed thoroughly before swallowing, the clench of his jaw as he ate drawing my attention to the strong curves of his face, the way dark stubble made the green of his eyes pop. The gulp of his throat was, in itself, somehow sexy. "Jacobs."

"Jacobs. Why the Bahamas, Mr. Jacobs?"

"Isn't that a question you should have asked me before you..."

I raised my eyebrows as he struggled for words. "Before I what?"

He met my playful gaze. "Trusted me with your body."

I shrugged. "Jena has your business card. She makes a practice of digging into every aspect of my life. I'm sure she has your blood type and latest draft of your résumé by this point. She hasn't called to warn me of anything, so I think my body is safe in your hands."

When his eyes darkened, they became hunter green. A heart-stopping change. Intensity looked incredible on this man. "I fish."

My eyes picked up on his tan, the flex of his forearms as he reached forward and snagged a piece of toast. I suddenly wanted to see him on the deck of a boat, wearing only swim trunks. The flex of his muscles as he battled a fish. The break of his smile when he caught a prize. I'd never seen him during the day. When the sun reflected in those eyes. I looked down, scooped up a spoonful of grits, and brought them to my mouth. Chewed. Swallowed. Looked back to find him watching me.

"Have you caught anything this trip?"

His mouth twitched. "Been too busy with a certain blonde to get any time in."

"Ahhh ... sure. Blame your bad luck on me." I shot him a look he found humorous, his mouth splitting into an easy grin.

I was digging out grapes from the fruit bowl when he spoke. "Stay a few more days with me."

I paused my quest for red ones. "I can't. I have work tomorrow." As I spoke the words I realized how out of character they were for me. Blaming work instead of the fact that staying here, with a stranger, was foolhardy. How strange that I wanted to stay. The warm buzz, the state of euphoria that seemed to accompany every moment in this man's presence ... it was a high I hadn't experienced in a long time. New love. Love that—at previous interactions—skipped along on its merry way after a few weeks. My last experience with this heady, butterflies in my tummy, elation in my heart feeling was ... high school? Back when I had fresh, unwounded eyes. Before I realized the selfishness and deceit that we, as adults, hold. The ugly truths of life that pull apart love and make our relationships obligation-centers that carry us from year to year, transition to transition.

"What do you do?"

His question brought me back. I popped an elusive red grape in my mouth before answering. "I'm a financial advisor. I work at a local bank in a town called Quincy."

"Why Quincy?"

I shrugged. "It's my hometown. After college I spent a few years in Athens with a guy I was dating. When that ended ... I didn't really have anywhere else to go. Didn't want to stay in Athens. So I came home." The super exciting story of my life. I changed the focus of the conversation. "What about you?"

He leaned back. "Fort Lauderdale. The bank can't do without you for a few days?"

I shook my head. "Nope. Why Fort Lauderdale? What do you do there?"

"I sell boats."

God, this guy was a regular chatterbox. I let my eyes float over the suite, the dining room table we seemed more likely to fuck on, the watch draped over his wallet, a brand I didn't recognize, but one I could guarantee was worth what I made in a year. "You sell boats."

He chuckled. "Yes." He slid over, pushing his tray forward, so close to the edge of the bed that I watched it nervously, my attention redirected when his lips closed over my neck. "Stop thinking," he whispered, taking another taste of my neck, this one more aggressive, one that would probably leave a hickey. Super classy, Riley. My mother would be thrilled. I closed my eyes. Leaned into his mouth. Let his arms slide my body up the bed and roll me atop him.

"I was overdramatic last night. What I said to you. About owning you."

"I figured it was for effect."

"But this isn't something I do. I don't make a habit of fucking strangers." His words tumbled awkwardly over the expletive, as if he wasn't used to swearing.

"Neither do I." Hell, I lived in a town where strangers didn't exist, and I *still* hadn't done any fucking. Showed what happened when I tried to brave life outside of our dirt roads.

"What are you doing next weekend?"

"Nothing." The lie came out convincingly. Kasey Craig, my second cousin on some distant family member's side, was actually having a baby shower on Saturday. Her fourth one in the last six years, yet there would be serious repercussions if I was not present. It is the South, after all. Not to mention, I also had plans to spray the yard for bugs. Super important stuff that my lie pushed to the side. I *wanted* this man. I knew little to nothing about him, but I craved something outside of my world. I was sick of pantyhose and mutual funds. Potluck dinners and familial obligations. This weekend was the most alive I'd felt in a decade. Part of it was the location; the majority of it had lay atop me. Had moved inside of me. Had woken me at 4 AM begging for five minutes inside of me, then blessed my world for twenty.

I was thirty-two. I was not dead. I was not in a relationship. I was bored. Had he asked me to pack up my house and move to Fort Lauderdale right now, I would have been tempted to say yes.

"See me next weekend. I'll send you a plane. It won't be the jet you girls flew in on, but it'll get you to me easier than commercial."

I looked at him. "How do you know what we came in on?"

"Don't get too excited. I was at the private airport when you arrived." He ran a hand through my hair. "Pretty blondes always catch my eye."

I let out a huff of air. "We're almost all blondes."

He smiled, that grin tugging hard at my vulnerable heart. "You leave them all in the dust."

The blush hot on my cheeks, I lifted my mouth, stopped from a kiss by his hand on my chest. "Next weekend?"

I smiled. "Maybe."

He shrugged. "I'll take it." His hand ran up my back, into my hair, his eyes softening as he studied me. Then, from beside us, the shrill screech of his phone. He let out an exasperated sigh. "Let me get that."

I rolled off him and watched him stand, the smooth swipe of his phone. He didn't check the display, just answered and held it to his ear. "Hey." He turned, giving me a wink as he opened the slider and stepped onto the balcony, the glass fitting snug as it closed, his words taken by the wind. I propped up on my elbows and studied him, the strong width of his back as he leaned against the railing, the break of his smile as he laughed. He huddled over the phone, cupping his hand over the receiver as if protecting it, the wind strong enough to tousle his hair and press his shirt flat against his chest.

I stared at him and felt my heart beating faster, my eyes tripping over the grip of his hand, the flap of his shirt. I wondered who he was talking to, out in the wind, this suite quiet and still. *Except for me.* Obviously, he went out for privacy. I yanked my eyes off him and swung my feet over the edge of the bed. He wanted to see me again, another weekend like this — one where we'd both pretend to be people we weren't and where I'd lose another piece of myself. He'd return to his life, and I'd have fallen a little deeper into the hole that was Brett Jacobs. I had the sudden, urgent desire to leave, to run from this man before goodbyes and false promises dirtied this memory. Better for me to leave now, while I had some tatters of dignity. While I could still pretend it was my choice. Look at me, the fun girl who bedded wild men and skipped out without a care in the world. I could play that girl, here in this empty room, with only a dirty room service tray to call my bluff. I scooped up my heels, checked for any forgotten items, then grabbed my cell and purse and slipped out the door.

chapter 11

tight (tīt)
(adj.) closely integrated and bound in love or friendship
"a tight-knit family"

Six girls on one jet was a disaster. We climbed in, elbows bumping armpits, suitcases unzipped on the pavement and last minute items grabbed before the pilot swung the luggage into the back. The plane belonged, like every other perk of the weekend, to Chelsea's dad. We'd used it a few times before: down to Panama City for spring break, up to Pennsylvania to ski. Enough times that we all had our place on the plane, jeans hitting seats with minimal arguments.

The door closed and there was one quiet moment before Megan, while pulling out her headphones, threw out the bone that started the conversation.

"Tammy says Riley didn't come home last night."

I groaned, pulling up my sweatshirt hood and slumping down in the seat, the neck-supporter doing little to ease the tension building. "Please. Don't act like you're sharing news that everyone hasn't already analyzed to death." *Why? Why did I have my one moment of slutdom right before a two-hour flight with them?*

"Well, you know *my* opinion on the subject."

A collective groan resonated through the cabin. Yes, we all knew Megan's opinion on the subject. The thirty-one-year-old virgin never missed a moment to voice her stance.

"Well, Megan, you sit there with your headphones and have a moment of silence to mourn the passing of Riley's celibacy," Chelsea said tartly. "I want *details*. I'm ten weeks away from being a one-penis woman."

"You've been a one-penis woman since tenth grade," Beth piped in from the back.

"Can we please stop calling Chelsea a "one-penis woman"? I'm getting sideshow visions." I closed the curtain beside me and wished this plane would freaking get going so we could have some airflow.

The door to the cockpit slid open and the co-pilot leaned back. *Great. With my luck, we're having engine trouble.* "I hate to bother you ladies, but there's a gentleman outside the plane."

We all shut up long enough to hear the bang of something against the door. Chelsea was the first to get her window curtain aside, my seat putting me on the wrong side of the plane. But I knew, as soon as her head snapped to me, who was outside. I closed my eyes for a brief moment. "Don't tell me..."

They didn't have to tell me. Mitzi worked the latch, the door swung up with a burst of sunlight, and I swear I could *smell* him, the scent of masculinity and possession as he strode up the stairs and pointed at me, his gorgeous mouth curving into a grin. "You. Outside. Unless you want me to kiss you senseless in front of all these ladies."

My glare's effect was weakened by the whoops of five women, a smattering of applause accompanying the cheers. I glanced at Chelsea, her dad's bill ticking higher with every minute we sat on the jetway. She tilted her head toward Brett, her eyes brimming with excitement, and moved her feet from the aisle. Rolling my eyes, I pushed off the armrests, my gaze drawing, without intent, to the delicious backside of Brett as he jogged down the plane's steps.

I plodded behind him, my tennis shoes heavy and slow. *What is he doing here? And why*—his shoes hit the ground and he turned, extending a hand out to me and tugging when I slid my palm into his. I made it down the last few steps, falling into his chest, his arms sliding up and wrapping around me. I looked up into his face. "Why are you—"

He silenced my question with his mouth, a firm kiss that he punctuated with action, his hands sliding down my arms and settling on my ass, squeezing the cheeks as if verifying his claim. "You left," he accused, pulling his mouth from mine and looking down, his words hard to focus on as he continued to grip my ass like he had every right.

"It was a fun weekend. No need to spoil it with false promises." I barely got out the words before he let go and dug in his pocket, my butt already missing the contact. I glanced up at the open door, curious faces darting away, Chelsea's big smile the only one to stay put. She watched without shame, my glare doing nothing to dissuade her. I'm shocked she didn't open some popcorn and prop up her feet.

"Here." He pressed something into my hand, and I looked down, a piece of hotel stationary folded in two, his number scribbled on the outside. "Call or text me when you get home safely, if you want. Or throw it away. It's in your court. But I couldn't let you leave without it."

I could feel the weight of the girls' stares, the tick of the clock as expensive minutes passed, the heat of the sun as it prickled the sunburnt tops of my shoulders. "I told you, this doesn't have to be anything."

"Or," he shrugged, stepping forward, his mouth pressing softly against my cheek, my lips crying for the missed contact, the taste of his tongue, the *onelastchance* that might have just flown by, "it could be the start of everything."

Then he stepped, one slow step back, then two, his hand reaching out, a casual wave given as his mouth broke open into a smile that would make Rob Lowe envious. "See ya, Riley."

I waved a slow hand, his number in between my fingers, fluttering in the wind, my hand dropping, closing tighter around the paper as I turned before he could and jogged up the steps of the plane. The door shut behind me, and I faced five seats of silent, curious eyes.

"Shut it," I blurted, dropping back into my seat and fastening the belt, my fingers shoving his number into my tote bag's inside pocket. "It was nothing."

"That, right there?" Tiny Beth stood, the pilot barking a protest, and pointed outside, all eyes craning to the windows. I didn't even want to know the view, didn't want to know what made a few squeals come from that general vicinity. "That was textbook romance. I'd give up an ovary for that right there."

Chelsea reached out and yanked at Beth's shirt, pulling her to her seat, the pilot finally turning back, the engines increasing in speed as

Every.

Eye.

Remained.

Locked.

On.

Me.

"Stop it," I warned, reclining the seat and stuffing the neck support back into place. "I had a one-night stand. End of story."

"Then you won't need his *number*."

I pried open one eye to see Beth reaching across the aisle, digging for my purse, Chelsea's booted heel catching her wrist and causing a shriek of pain.

"Before Riley shares all the juicy secrets about her night of passion, let me give you ladies the rundown on Mr. Brett Jacobs." Jena's voice crowed from behind me.

"I'm not sharing any juicy secrets," I interjected. I pulled the purse out of reach, sandwiching it between my calves, and closed my eyes, feigning disinterest.

Jena didn't pause, the trajectory of her voice indicating a rise in position, the blonde no doubt holding court and relishing every moment of it. "Brett Jacobs is listed on Betschart Yachts' website as being a sales manager, his job description consists of ... well, he's a salesman," she finished plainly. "But of big-ticket items. Their cheapest yacht starts at ten million, which…" At her pause, there was a flutter of papers. Good God, the woman probably had a PowerPoint presentation at the ready. "Which, if I estimate just a percentage of commission, we're talking six figures per boat." There was an impressed hum of approval from the group, and I willed her to shut up. The plane moved forward, and some of my hair got caught in the fresh grip of her hand on my headrest. I winced, reaching a hand back and carefully pulled my ponytail free, the action discovering a wealth of knots and bumps along the top of my head. Great ... messy hair. Way to make a lasting impression.

"Married?" Megan piped up.

"According to the Florida Marriage Records, nope. That same database clears him, or any other Brett Jacobs, of any crimes, convictions, or warrants. He's good."

"He looks pretty *old* to have never been married." That was Chelsea, the voice coming from my right.

"Well, I couldn't find an exact age ... I couldn't find much of anything, really. Riley?" Jena's voice softened on my name, and I felt her hand lighten, the woman probably peering over me like a hungry bird to a worm. I let out a deep sigh that closely resembled a snore and hoped this conversation would end soon.

"Ms. Crawford, we're up next for takeoff, please buckle." I peeked out of the bottom of my eyelids at the pilot who glared at Jena as if she would actually listen. Shockingly, I felt my seat snap back into place as she huffed into her seat, the click of her belt reassuring me of at least a brief interlude of peace.

Minutes later, the plane vibrating with the force of our departure, we were airborne, and everyone's conversations moved to other gossip. I kept my eyes closed, my mouth slightly ajar, and faked sleep until the moment we landed.

I didn't know what to think about the man, his number, or our night. But I did—as I sat in my car in the airport parking lot, the radio gently playing, the girls leaving one-by-one from either side of me— pull out my phone and send a text message to the number on the paper.

We made it safely. I'm home now.

I hesitated before pressing SEND, not sure what else to say. I felt as if I should thank him ... but for what? We had sex. Slept some. Screwed some more. He gave me breakfast. I ran out. Maybe I should thank him for breakfast. I typed the words, then deleted them, my cursor making a hurried backtrack over the letters. I pressed SEND before I could think about it anymore, then tossed my phone into the passenger seat and drove home. Halfway there, at a four-way stop in the middle of cornfields, I picked it back up. Read his response.

Sleep well beautiful. My bed feels empty.

My bed feels empty? What a random ass thing to say. I stared at the text. Random ass and impossible to respond to. I rolled down the window and had the strong urge to chuck the phone as far into the dried stalks as it would go. The other half of me wanted to preserve the screen under glass *forever*. I was a complete head case. I thought having sex would clear out the cobwebs and help me think. Instead, I couldn't function, my brain and thought process tied into knots that spelled out Brett.

I rolled up the window, turned off the damn phone, and swore I'd stop thinking of him for the rest of the night. It wouldn't lead to anything, I knew it. Maybe one more trip, one more stab to my heart before he disappeared forever. Nothing to get excited or vulnerable about. I was me and he was *him* and he'd forget about me by Monday. It had been a fun weekend but I'd probably never hear from him again.

chapter 12
Kitten

"You don't get to tell me to stop. I am the only one with that power. The only thing I will grant you is the ability to ask for more. To beg."

"I will never beg for you. Not in the way you are asking."

"Oh ... Kitten. You have no idea."

"Don't call me that."

In the cell, there were no books, no television. I had a stack of blank journals, nothing else. During my first few weeks I wrote in them. Once I realized that he read them, flipped through my pages, copied excerpts into his book, I stopped. I could hold onto my memories and thoughts without giving him a front-row seat to my truths. Instead, I used the pages to draw, to illustrate pieces of my past life that would make sense to only me. My sketches started out rudimentary, crude doodles of my friends, parents, a flower I grew once in a kitchen pot. But, with unlimited time devoted to my new hobby, I improved. Grew more detailed. More lifelike. Once, I earned a pack of colored pencils, so the sketches began to contain bits of greens and yellows, blues and pinks. I tried to ration them, too proud to ask for more.

Occasionally, if a sketch was particularly good, I destroyed it. Ripped off a piece at a time, letting the bits collect in a pile before I scooped them into my hand and let them flutter into the toilet. Flushed and watched the colorful fragments of evidence swirl away. It was a self-protective measure, verification that I was not placing too much happiness, too much identity in those pages. The more I cared, the sharper the edge of the item, the bigger the weapon I handed over for him to hurt me. In that room, in that environment, he was eager for shards, pieces of my heart to poke at and record the reaction.

It was why I flushed the paper.

It was why I never mentioned Brett to him.

chapter 13

I was at my desk, a collection of client files stretched out before me, when my cell buzzed.

Hey beautiful.

I picked it up. Stared at the words, then moved hesitant thumbs.

hey

I had a great time this weekend.

Agreed. Thanks for...

I bit my lip, my fingers hovering over the keypad. Thanks for what? The smoking hot sex? The resetting of my prude-o-meter? The reminder of everything my current life is missing? I deleted the words.

Agreed.

I pressed send and watched the curtest response ever sail off into cyberspace.

When can I see you again?

just stop

what?

It was fun, but we live a thousand miles apart. It won't work.

my map search says it's 410 miles

My lip bite became less about indecision and more about holding back my smile. I locked my phone and tossed it onto the desk before I made a stupid decision and sent a text that would get me further into trouble. That was him. Trouble. I rolled forward and picked up my office phone. Dialed a number and waited for Mitzi to answer. Ignored the text alert buzz of my cell and swore to myself that I wouldn't touch it. Not for — I glanced at the clock — at least fifteen minutes.

"Hey," Mitzi's snap into the phone interrupted my reach for my cell.

"Hey. Talk me off this ledge."

"I assume this ledge you speak of is Island Boy?" In the background there was the clatter of pots and the shrill scream of a child. "Shit. Just a second." I heard her scream, threats were made, and then she was back, not even a little breathless.

"Yeah, that ledge." I spun a pen on my desk.

"Jump, woman. Jump with both feet and arms outstretched and pretty-fucking-please take me with you when you fall." The smile in her words didn't belie the truth I heard in the request.

"It's stupid." I started the debate we'd already had three times since Monday night.

"Who cares?" *That* was the issue. My arguments had merit, and hers were that of a fourth-grade shouting match.

"We live too far away."

"So?"

"I don't even know him."

"Yet. But you can."

"You suck at this."

"I'm not gonna stand in the way of what could be true love."

My next spin was a little too aggressive, and the Bic shot toward the edge of the desk. There was a rap on the glass of my wall and I looked up, raising my eyebrows when I saw what was there. "Mitzi, I'm getting flowers."

"Bitch, God is smacking you on the damn forehead. Jump."

I heard the click on her end and slowly hung up the receiver, gesturing in a kid, one who looked barely out of high school. I stood, watching warily as he carefully set the vase down, the entire arrangement tipping slightly before it found solid footing. "Thanks."

"No problem, ma'am. They sure are big."

I nodded, reaching out and snagging the card, the boy's eyes following. I set it on my desk, my hand covering it. "Thanks." I repeated the sentiment, and he finally turned, nodding to me with a smile and moving to the door. I tapped the card against the desk before letting out a sigh and flipping it over.

I can't get you out of my head.

I stared at the words until they blurred, and I tossed the card down, my butt settling deeper into my chair as I leaned back and looked at the flowers, a huge display of orchids and lilies, a colorful blend that brought me back to the island without even trying. He couldn't get me out of his head? The feeling was mutual. Then, after a good ten minutes spent analyzing the decision, I picked my phone back up. Skimmed over his last text.

take a chance.

I took a deep breath, then responded.

I'm free this weekend.

chapter 14

5 months, 3 weeks before

My first passport stamp ever had been for that bachelorette party. And, just a week later, I was getting a second. I flipped my passport closed and tossed the navy book into my bag, zipping closed my suitcase, the contents already over-analyzed at least a dozen times.

"You'll be fine," Jena drawled from the kitchen, as she waltzed into my bedroom with two glasses of sweet tea. "Here. Take these. We don't want you vomiting on Island Boy's plane."

"I don't get airsick," I responded, my stomach flipping as the words came out. Maybe I *could* get airsick. I took the pills from her and sat on the edge of the bed. Tossed back the medicine and took a deep sip of tea. Winced. "Did you get this from the fridge?"

"Yeah."

I grabbed her wrist and stopped her mid-sip. "Don't drink that. It's old."

"Old, Monday? Or old, last month?"

I groaned, took the glass away. "It's *old*. I'll just grab us beers."

She followed me into the kitchen, glancing at her watch. "Better make 'em sodas. You've got to leave in twenty to make it to the airport on time."

"Is it too late to cancel?" I dumped out the glasses, then opened the fridge and grabbed two Cokes, tossing one her way.

"I thought Mitzi talked to you about this. She's the convincer, not me."

"Which is why I wanted you here. Is this crazy?"

"You running off to a foreign country with a man you barely know? Yes." Jena cracked open her Coke and held it to her forehead. "It's hot in here. Did you already turn off the air?"

"Turn on the fan. I'm trying to lower the utility bill. So ... I shouldn't go?"

She plopped down at my round table, picking through my mail until she found a postcard with enough strength to act as a fan. "It's crazy, but I didn't say you shouldn't go. Go. Live. Hell, one person in this town should do something exciting. I'm saddled with two kids and a husband who hasn't gone down on me since prom night. I'd kill for two nights in Aruba with a sexy stranger. Just be smart. What's your dad think?"

I looked away. "Haven't told him. But I'm sure word'll reach him by the time I return. If he calls you, let him know you have my hotel info and Brett's number in case of emergency."

She groaned. "Great. Put *me* in the line of fire."

"You're the only one who'll stand up to him. The other girls will hand over the information as soon as he starts yelling."

She stood. "You know I love you, right?"

I smiled. "I know. Thanks for feeding Miller."

"Gives me an excuse to escape the kids. Sleep in your bed. Watch your porn."

I laughed. "You find any, please leave it out for me. Showtime's the only excitement these walls have seen lately."

She held out her arms. "Gimme a hug, then get out of here."

I gripped her tightly. "Wish me luck."

"You don't need it."

***

I climbed onto the plane, a miniature version of Chelsea's, with propellers instead of jets, with four seats behind the cockpit's two.

Brett crawled in behind me, a cell to his ear, the moment before takeoff stolen as he wrapped up a conversation. I was grateful, unsure what to say, feelings of awkwardness at an all-time high. I'd have to sleep with him, right? The man flew here, picked me up, and was taking me to Aruba? It'd be assumed, especially since our prior encounter had revolved around ripped panties and orgasms and ohmygodIthinkIsuckedhisdick. I looked around for a vomit bag and didn't see one. Clenched my hands around the handle of my purse and felt the leather bend.

"You okay?" He was off the phone, his hand settling on my shoulder, and I jumped a little at the contact, my gaze tripping to him, his eyes concerned, brows furrowed. God, he was even more beautiful than I remembered. I was a great girl ... but ... I was small-town pretty. Didn't even own a thong till the bachelorette party. I wore a retainer to bed. Snored. Had the coordination of a giraffe. Barely owned two pairs of socks that matched. Shopped for clothes at Walmart. I didn't belong on a private plane with this man, whose five o'clock shadow could dominate a magazine cover.

"I'm sorry, Riley. I didn't realize you were afraid of flying." He fished under his seat, produced a paper bag. "It seems cliché, but breathe into this. It'll help."

Thank God. A flimsy vessel for my throw-up. I grabbed the bag and opened it with shaky hands. Held it over my mouth, breathed deeply, and checked my stomach for queasiness. Yep, still there.

"Do you want to wait? We don't need to take off. I can run inside, see if there's a bigger plane I can charter."

I shook my head. "I'll be fine," I managed to say, the words muffled a little by the bag. "It's just nerves."

When he reached across me, his hands gently searching for, and pulling out, the seatbelt, I inhaled. Got a whiff of his cologne that took me back to last weekend.

I feel the rough prickle of his cheek, wet suction as my right nipple makes its way into his mouth, his soft play of tongue against

*delicate skin, probing and teasing, a low moan coming out of me
when he gently bites the tip of it.*

Okay, I could do this. I was a big girl. The edge of his hands
brushed against my bare thighs, my sundress pushed up by my seated
position. He glanced my way, his breath pausing slightly, and when
our gazes met it was all I could do to keep my legs still, to not open
them, the final movement of his hands - clenching, then tightening my
belt - done with his eyes on mine, our mouths just inches apart, the
bag dropping from my hand as I stared at him.

"Thank you for coming this weekend." He let go of my belt, one
hand settling on my bare knee. I felt every finger of that touch, five
hot points of contact that seared through my skin and lit a path
directly upward.

I swallowed. "Thank you for inviting me."

He didn't smile, didn't acknowledge, just moved his fingers in a
slight caress. I inhaled and put my hand on top of his. "Unless you
plan on doing something with that hand, please stop. I literally can't
think straight."

He laughed and his breath smelled like peppermints. "I'm trying
to distract you. From the takeoff."

Oh. We were taking off. I curled my fingers around his hand and
he tightened it a little on my knee.

"And.. we're off." He tilted his head to the window, and I
glanced over, the rumble beneath us quieted. I felt his hand move
underneath mine.

I bit the inside of my cheek. "I wasn't scared of flying. The
nerves were more about us. This weekend."

He frowned. "I didn't mean to pressure you to come."

I smiled. "It's a weekend in *Aruba*. I'll survive."

"If it's the sex that worries you, we don't have to. You take the
lead on that."

"Okay." I spoke quickly, before my pacifist side denied the
request.

"Good." He reached back out, squeezed my hand. "You still need the bag?" Reaching down, he plucked the crumpled brown paper off the carpeted floor.

"No, I think I'm good."

I rolled my hand over, looped my fingers through his, and felt myself begin to relax.

chapter 15

In the hotel lobby, I stared down at my key, the marble floor below framing it in waves of tan, and tried to fit this piece into the puzzle that was Brett. This was *my* key. He held his, for a *different* room, and signed the bill, the front desk clerk all but climbing over the counter in her attempts to flirt with him.

When he stepped away, reaching for my hand, I held up the key. "We didn't have to get separate rooms."

He stopped, the two of us in the wide expanse of the lobby, the ocean glinting at me behind the glass. "It was presumptuous to assume anything else."

Presumptuous. I'd be willing to bet I'd never heard a prospective boyfriend use that word before. I shrugged. "I mean ... we're adults. We can share a bed without having sex." God, what an awkward and unnecessary conversation. Why was my mouth still moving? Why didn't I shut up and stuff the key in my purse like a good girl?

He chuckled. "Let me be a gentleman. Please."

I shrugged, sticking my key in my purse. Yes, Riley. Let the man be a gentleman. I followed him into the elevator.

Ding.

Ding.

The damn car just had to ding with every floor, a sound that only made the silence between us more obvious. Brett coughed. I played with the leather fringe of my key chain. I should have left my keys at home, or in the glove box of my car. My luck, I'd lose them in Aruba and be screwed. *Screwed.* I felt an adolescent giggle swell in my throat.

The doors opened. Third floor. I stepped out, he followed, and this awkward carnival moved down the hall. My key card worked, he opened the door, and I stepped inside.

Wow. I'd been expecting a traditional hotel room, but this one had two bathrooms, a sitting area off the bedroom, and a balcony that overlooked the oceanfront pool. I looked down, verified that it was, in fact, my key that had opened the door. If this was my room, I couldn't imagine his.

"You like it?" Brett stood in the doorway, his own key flipping through his hands.

I nodded with a smile. "Yeah, I like it."

"The bellman will bring up your bag. How much time do you need before dinner?"

I shrugged. "Five minutes?"

The corner of his mouth turned up. "Five minutes ... how low maintenance of you."

"It's less about that, more about my hunger."

He laughed at that, tapping his card against his leg. "Okay. In that case, I'll wait here. Let you change and then we can go." He pulled out his cell, gestured to the balcony. "I just need to make some calls."

"Go for it." Behind him, a bellman appeared, and I waved him in. Watched him set out my bags as Brett stepped to the railing, the glass door closing behind him, his phone out. So identical to last weekend, yet so different. Before, with him outside, I'd had a hundred doubts, had felt out of place and only wanted to escape. Now, I felt similar unease, but it was more over his actions than mine. Why was I being weird about having my own room? He was being polite, a gentleman, giving me my own space, one without pressure or expectations. It was just ... our prior meetings had been so passionate and quick, his hands—once we'd entered the room—grabbing me with such need that there'd been no doubt about his desire. This Brett, the one settled in a balcony chair, had such control, such patience. It calmed my nerves, but poked holes in any confidence I'd had in my sexual allure.

***

Any awkwardness dissolved in the hotel's restaurant, an oceanfront palace that felt fancy until I saw the maître'd's flip-flops at the base of his seersucker suit.

"Favorite movie?" I spun the Corona bottle cap, watching it flip off the table and onto the sandy deck.

"*Shawshank Redemption*."

"Ugh." I took a swig of beer. "That's every man's favorite movie. Pick another."

"It's every man's favorite movie because it's incredible."

"Pick another. And..." I tilted my head. "It's got to involve a main character singing."

He scrunched his face at me. "You want my favorite movie, and it has to involve *that*?"

"Yep." I dipped a carrot into crab dip and crunched half of it into my mouth. "First date rules. You have to do whatever I say."

"This is our first date? What about—"

I wave him off. "The Bahamas didn't count."

"Okay... I'll follow your first date rules if you follow my first night rules."

"Which are?" I narrowed my eyes at him, though I couldn't stop the hint of a smile.

"You have to do whatever I say."

"Hmm ... sounds kinky." I raised my eyebrows at him and took another sip of Corona. "Thought that ball was in my court?"

He shrugged. "You're a woman. That ball is always in your court."

"Fine. Deal." I sat back, the waitress clearing our bread plates with quick efficiency. "Ma'am, can we get two shots of Patron please?"

"Tequila?" Brett asked, leaning back in his seat, the gap from the table a perfect depth for me to straddle his legs. I busied myself with a crab leg instead.

"You're evading. Favorite movie with impromptu singing."

"*The Wedding Singer.*"

"Nope. He was a singer, so that doesn't count."

"So ... Johnny Cash, Elvis, Rockstar... those don't count?"

"Nope. Nope. Nope."

"*Jerry Maguire.*"

I put down the crab leg, snapping my eyes to his. Oh my word, he just got even hotter. He grinned. "You approve?"

I laughed. "Yes. I approve. I was expecting something more manly, like *Top Gun* or *Full Metal Jacket*, but I approve."

He winced. "How did I miss those?"

"I complete you," I said with a wink.

The alcohol made the comeback hilarious, and we were wheezing by the time the disapproving waiter brought our entrees.

***

"I like watching you eat." Brett wiped his mouth and leaned back, setting the white cloth napkin next to his plate. Five desserts covered the surface between us, bites missing from each. We'd done a horrible job of finishing, but a great job of sampling.

"Good. I like to eat." I winked at him and stretched back, straightening my legs beneath the table.

"You are a very sexy eater. Has anyone ever told you that?"

I laughed. "Sexy eater ... hmm. Never got that compliment before." My exes, bless their hearts, weren't suave enough to know how much compliments were appreciated. I had been lucky to get a 'You're pretty' on a date. "Think I should add it to my Match.com profile?"

His eyes hardened, and he leaned forward, his elbows settling on the table. "Oh no. I can think of much better adjectives than that."

"Really?" I widened my eyes dramatically and was momentarily distracted by the key lime pie. Maybe one more bite … no. My stomach was officially full. "Please share."

"Let's see." He looked down, the fingers of his left hand rubbing thoughtfully over his mouth. *His knuckles are scarred.* I hadn't noticed that before, the table's candle flickering over faded thin lines, like he had punched a hundred walls. Such a contrast to the controlled man before me. "You have horrible taste in sensible footwear. Prefer high-pressure sexual advances to gentlemanly overtures. Can order a poor man into bankruptcy. Have questionable judgment when it comes to choosing travel companions."

I twisted my mouth in an attempt not to smile. "I think those things are bad. The point is to highlight my strengths."

"Oh no." He shook his head, leaning back in his seat. "We can't do that. If we tried to list your attractive qualities, we'd run out of space."

I laughed, feeling my cheeks heat. I should be better at this. Should probably cross my legs and lean forward, putting my breasts on display. Grin knowingly, like I received swoon-worthy comments every day. Should toss my hair and look natural doing it.

"So how is your online search for true love coming?" He raised his eyebrows with interest.

"Horribly," I groaned. "Which may be due to the fact that my town's dating pool is only about a hundred people deep. I think I have to expand the search area."

"Or close it entirely."

We weren't having the 'exclusive' talk right then. It was impossible. Too soon. I shrugged. Leaned forward and took another look at the deliciousness that was the key lime pie. Maybe I could have *one* more bite.

"Looks like a whole lotta deep thought going on over there," Brett remarked, scribbling his signature on the bill.

"Not really. Just trying to resist temptation." I looked up and smiled wryly.

"Me too." The right side of his mouth pulled up, revealing the dimple in his cheek. He really *was* gorgeous. Heartbreakingly so. "Ready?" He stood and offered his hand.

"Ready." I took it and stood, his hand linking through mine, our stroll back to the room a leisurely journey. Beside us, the ocean glittered in the moonlight, the crash of waves delicately quiet in the backdrop. I wondered if he'd try something once we got to my room. I was almost woozy from the food, the wine with dinner putting me in a wistful state of calm.

We came to a stop next to the elevator, and he pressed the button. Wrapped his hand around my back and pulled me into his chest. "Your hair smells so good," he murmured, putting a soft kiss on the top of it.

"Good-smelling hair. Seductive eater ... keep going Mr. Jacobs," I whispered, lifting my chin from his chest to look up at him.

"Oh no. I'm not giving your online dating any more of a boost," he grumbled, the chime of the elevator breaking our moment.

I laughed and let him pull me inside the lift, his hands pulling me back against him as soon as the doors closed.

chapter 16

"Girl, this better be worth international minutes," Chelsea, the only one of my friends who could *afford* international minutes, huffed into the receiver, the drone of the treadmill running on slow in the background.

"It's really not, but talk to me anyway."

"What, the sex sucks?"

"Haven't had any yet."

"What?" Her screech was so loud I had to pull my cell away from my ear. "It's been two days!"

"Twenty-nine hours," I corrected mildly. "*And* we're in separate rooms."

"Why?"

I fished an earring out of my makeup bag, blowing at the front of it in an attempt to remove cotton ball fuzz. "I don't know. I was nervous on the plane; I think he is trying to be respectful. Not push."

"You already boned the guy. What more does he want?"

I groaned. Maybe Chelsea was the wrong person to call. "Last night we got trashed. He brought me to my room and tucked me in."

"And today?"

I glanced at the clock. "Flowers were delivered this morning, along with a note for me to call him when I woke up."

"So call him."

"I just want to know what this is. What I'm getting into."

"Holy cheese balls. Just fuck the guy. Dance on the beach. Have fun for the first time ever. It all doesn't have to be a five-year plan with an amortization schedule."

I blinked. Not to be offensive, but I didn't even realize Chelsea *knew* what an amortization schedule was. But she had a point. I was approaching middle age. Single. On an island with a man whose mere touch made me shiver. I should be riding him like a prized stallion.

"You're right. Let me run." I hung up the phone and fell back on the bed. Rolled over different scenarios in my mind with the aggression of an eighty-year-old woman. Did I have the balls to seduce? Make a move? Or should I just wait until tonight? I stood and walked over to his flowers. A beautiful arrangement. One that would be wasted, our departure a scant twenty-four hours away. *Twenty-four hours left in paradise.* And I was sitting alone in the room when I could be repeating last weekend's orgasmic glory. What *was* I doing? At the very least I should follow his request and call. Let him know I was awake. Or … I could follow Chelsea's directive. Jumping into his bed seemed like a lot more fun. A lot more daring. A lot more like the woman I'd like to one day become.

I walked to the bathroom and undid my robe. Looked at my naked body in the mirror. Turned right, then left, then right. Leaned forward, checked my teeth. Brushed my teeth. Used mouthwash. Returned to the room and laid on the carpet. Did a dozen crunches before I realized the futility of trying at this point. Got dressed in my lingerie set, purchased three days earlier at Quincy's local department store. Stood in front of the mirror again. Right, left, right. Realized how ridiculous I looked in red lace and garters. Stripped again. Pulled the robe back on and cinched it tight. Avoided the bathroom mirror and found Brett's room number. Had a mini panic attack. Downed a tiny bottle of rum from the minibar. Decided to brush my teeth again. Grimaced at the combination of mint and rum. Called Chelsea back and regained my resolve. Rode the elevator up two more floors and knocked on Brett's door.

When he answered the door, I stepped inside. Dug my hands into the cotton of his shirt and pushed him back, against the wall, his hands fast on the tie of my robe, a groan rumbling from his mouth when he yanked it open and saw my naked body. Our mouths stole a hundred kisses in a few minutes, short frantic ones, long, deep discoveries, a blur of tongues and teeth and *moremoremore*. And suddenly, all was right. It was instant, hot freaking passion that didn't leave room for nerves or awkwardness. It was the prior weekend all over again, and I dragged my fingers through his hair, twisted in it, his hands exploring the skin underneath my robe. I felt the pull of his palms on my ass as he yanked me closer, one hand sliding down ... down the crack of my ass, over the pucker of skin and to the wet slit, a place where - when he pushed inside - we both reacted, my body curving closer, wanting more, his mouth coming off me to gasp out my name.

"Pull me out," he said, his hands occupied, one finger slowly dipping in, then out, in, then out, then ... two fingers. His other hand, on the back of my neck, curled in my hair, kept me close. When I arched against him, his eyes drank it in, eager and greedy, and if I could bottle up that moment, I would never have to wonder if he found me attractive. I could open it and sip it, a bit at a time, and be satisfied my whole life. But that devouring of me with his eyes? It was gas on my fire, and my hands shook as I ripped at his belt, jerked on his zipper, and ... finally, a day too late ... palmed and pulled out his cock.

chapter 17
Kitten

tight (tīt)
(adj.) allowing little or no room for free motion or movement

The man who kept me had an accent, a thick coating over every word, something I might have found sexy in another life. Now, in this one, I wanted to cut out his tongue and never hear another of his affected syllables.

He sat before me, my hands again tied, this time to the lower cuffs, a more comfortable position. My bare ass sat in the wooden chair, my ankles secured to the legs of it. I tried to fall over, tried to rip the chair, but only succeeded in wrenching my opposing arm practically out of socket.

Now, my bones tired, throat sore from screaming, I sat and tried to block out the words that he spoke.

"Do you know that in the UK a sex slave ring of 1,400 victims was just discovered? It's the fifth one of its kind, led by Muslim men, that has been found. I find it fascinating that they target white women, such as you. Do you know why, Kitten?"

I didn't respond, my eyes avoiding his, focusing on the pad of paper he held on his lap, his pen tapping the surface with a quick rat-a-tat-tat that was driving me crazy.

"They say that if the ethnicity of the victim and abuser are different, then the crime seems less severe. It's a mental Band-Aid, really, to the victim. That's why I was so pleased to get you, Kitten. To see if I felt less empathy for you. Now, I'm wondering if it works in reverse. If you feel less empathy and connection to me, as your Master."

"You're not my Master." The words spilled out before I could contain them, and I watched his pen as it stopped its tap and swiveled upright.

"Well then, what would you call me? The majority of sex traffickers in the United States are prostitution rings, in which the Master is called 'Daddy.' Would you prefer that name, Kitten?"

I looked up from his pen, into his eyes. "No. And I'm not Kitten."

He chuckled, the corner of his mouth drawing up as if pulled by a thread, his eyes tight on mine like he found me fascinating. "I use the nickname to help you forget your old life. Also, it is a form of endearment. Most slaves embrace their new names."

"How many have you dealt with?" I asked the question quietly, unsure of his reaction, my hate of this man one-upped by my fear of him.

"Well ... just you so far. If you don't give me what I need, then I'll have to get another. Which takes me to the second part of today's training." He set his clipboard aside and my breath stalled, my chest tightening as I prepared for the unknown.

chapter 18

5 months, 1 week before

The man had the art of courtship down. I wondered, as I sat at my desk and opened the box, how many times he had done this. How many women he had courted from afar, how many companions he had flown to every Caribbean island. Wondered, not for the first time, if I was a mistress and playing second fiddle to a Mrs. Jacobs.

The box was chocolate brown, with a red satin ribbon, and had arrived at the bank this morning via UPS. I'd cut open the ordinary brown box and there sat this, nestled in a sea of Styrofoam peanuts, its bow perfectly in place despite the shipping. I'd shut the box before anyone saw it and carried it into my office, kicking the door shut and bumping it with my butt until it clicked into place.

Now I pulled off the ribbon and opened the lid, with no idea of what it could contain. I laughed when I parted monogrammed tissue paper, the top item being a pair of slippers, much like the ones he had first given me, but these were embroidered with my name, in delicate script along the top. I set them aside and reached deeper, pulling out a matching robe, "Riley" also present there, on the breast pocket, a pale blue card peeking out of it. I pulled out the card, Betschart Yachts embossed in gold at the top.

You seem to be fond of robes and slippers. Hoping to see you naked of both soon.

I blushed and set aside the robe, my eye catching on a gold-wrapped package at the bottom of the box. A gift inside a gift. I reached in and pulled it out, the box small and rectangular. Too big for jewelry, too small for a book. I ripped open the packaging and found a phone, a brand I'd never seen. An Iridium, black and bulky, with actual buttons instead of a touch screen. A post-it was taped to the box's front with *Call me, I'll explain* written in what I now recognized as Brett's handwriting.

I picked up my desk phone and dialed his cell. Swiveled in the chair so that my back was to the branch and flipped the phone box over, reading its features on the back.

"Hey beautiful." His voice was warm, the background quiet. I smiled.

"Hey. I just got a box of gifts."

"You deserve them every day. I've been slacking off. Didn't want to scare you off." There was a smile in his words, and I laughed.

"You do know that I have a phone already."

"And you should keep it. That one is for when you travel. It's built for international use; it's a satellite phone."

"Meaning...?" Two weeks earlier, I'd have hidden my ignorance. Now, I felt at ease.

"Meaning that it'll pick up a signal anywhere. I don't want you to be out of touch with your friends and family."

I blinked. It was, for a guy, surprisingly ... thoughtful. "Thank you. That's really nice of you." I had actually planned to refuse the gift. I did, after all, have my own phone. A perfectly nice iPhone, which – twenty minutes earlier – had seemed overly adequate for my limited needs.

"You're welcome. Don't give me too much credit. I do have ulterior motives."

"Don't all men?" I teased.

He laughed. "The second weekend of July, there's a fishing event I'm attending. I'd love to take you there by boat. It'll be in the middle of nowhere; you'll need that phone."

The middle of nowhere … it sounded so ominous. I'd never fully gotten over a stranded-at-sea movie I'd watched in fifth grade. "We'd boat from Fort Lauderdale?"

Another chuckle. "No, you probably don't have enough time for that. We'd fly into Puerto Rico. Take the boat from there."

I spun to my computer. Pulled up Google Maps. Quickly realized why boating from Fort Lauderdale would be impossible. Then I moved to my desk calendar and looked with despair at my schedule. Even nine weeks out, it was full.

"I'd have to work a full day on Friday. *And* be back at work on Monday," I said glumly.

"I'll make it work. The plane can pick you up Friday night and have you back late Sunday."

"You sure?" I leaned back, closing the browser window. Picking up the robe, I ran my hand over the soft fleece. It would easily be the nicest thing I'd ever worn.

"Absolutely. Is it a date?"

I closed my eyes and rested my head against the back of the chair. "It's a date."

"Talk to you tonight?"

I smiled. "Yes."

I didn't realize until after I hung up the phone, a ridiculous smile still on my face, that I hadn't thanked him for the slippers and robe. I repacked the box, tying the ribbon back into place, my bow not looking nearly as nice as the original one, and made a mental note to thank him during our phone call that night.

chapter 19

"Ooooh…" Tammy's squeal could put a pig in heat. I widened my eyes at her, and she went silent, instead waving her hands in excitement. "That is so romantic!" she whispered loudly, leaning forward across the table at me.

"Good Lord, Tammy, he *bought* something, he didn't slay a dragon and rescue her from a castle," Jena grumbled, swatting my hands away from the onion ring appetizer she was refusing to share.

"Shut it, Jena. It's romantic. When's the last time Matt got you anything?"

Ouch. Low blow. My wide eyes turned to a warning glare, and I kicked at Tammy under the table. Matt worked on one of the Vance's tobacco farms. They covered their bills, they didn't spoil each other with gifts. But Jena only shrugged good-naturedly. "I'm just saying … it's a phone. It's not romantic. It's random."

"I think it's thoughtful." I didn't bother pointing out the robe and slippers, which I thought were romantic, especially given our history with the items. If Jena wanted to think it was a dumb gift … whatever. She was a big girl with her own opinions, just like me.

"It's weird. He probably just wants to control you. Be able to see who you call since his name's on the bill. In fact … wait a minute." She put down a half-eaten ring, and I swiped it. "Lemme see the phone?"

I raised an eyebrow at her, reaching into my bag and digging around for it. "I haven't charged it yet. And it doesn't have Bejeweled. I already checked." Jena is, and she'll let you know it early on, the county's reigning champion at Bejeweled. We all play it; she dominates it. Her high score's up in the twenty-million-point range.

She looked at the box, pulling out her own phone and searching for something on the Internet. "Ha!" she spat out the word like she'd found the cure for cancer.

"What?" Tammy took the bait, reaching for the box, which Jena held out of reach.

"The Iridium 9555 *can be easily tracked*, making it a favorite among survivalists and emergency personnel," Jena read from her phone with loud authority, the entire right side of Ruby Tuesday hearing every syllable.

"Would you *be quieter*," I hissed. "Between the two of you, Roy will kick us out."

"Shut up, he will *not*." Jena waved her hand in the general direction of the manager, her voice managing to drop to a more reasonable level as she set down her cell. "Did you hear me, Riley? His romantic gift is allowing him to track you."

"I think half the restaurant heard you," Tammy supplied the words before I could.

"Did *you* even listen to yourself?" I cut in. "The tracking isn't for crazy boyfriends. It's for *emergency* situations. Which is probably why most people have a satellite phone in the first place. I'm not using the thing walking around Quincy. I'm using it when I'm out of town. With him. To talk to you guys."

"She's right," Tammy chimed in. "You're being crazy, Jena."

"I'm being cautious," Jena growled. "Forgive me if I'm not jumping on the I-Love-Brett bandwagon that you all are intent on decorating."

"Hey, you're the one who told me to go to Aruba, remember?" I reached out, taking the last onion ring out of pure spite. "You stood in my living room and all but pushed me out the door."

"For *one* trip! I didn't think it would *lead* anywhere!" Jena glared at me, and I tried to figure out what she was really saying. Why she was against this … relationship, or whatever you wanted to call what Brett and I were doing. I stared back at her and her eyes softened. Then she slumped back in her booth. "I just don't want you to get hurt, Ril. He *does* seem great. *Too* great. There's got to be something wrong."

It was sad that that was how we thought. I *knew* what she was saying. I felt the same way. This couldn't be happening. He couldn't be attracted to me. Still interested in me. Setting dates six weeks out. I felt like I was in a glass house and waiting for a giant to step on it. Crush my blissful happiness in a horrific moment that would feel, in small part, like a blessing. Because it would have finally arrived, and the waiting, the horrible anticipation would be over, finally I wouldn't have to wonder, I would *know*, unequivocally, that this fairytale had ended, and my normal life could resume its plod through normalcy.

"You can't protect me," I said quietly. "I can't even do that."

"I know," she said. "But I hate it."

I leaned forward and gripped her hand. "And I love you for it."

"And me?" Tammy piped in, worry lacing her words. Jena and I laughed, and she threw her arm around Tammy.

"And you," I reassured her. "I love you guys."

chapter 20

4 months, 2 weeks before
Puerto Vallarta, Mexico

We laid back to front, his leg wrapped around me, every inch of us touching, the dark room illuminated in waves from the images on the screen. Before us, the final scene of *Romeo & Juliet*.

"Have you ever loved someone like that? Where you'd have given your life for her?" I whispered the words through the dark, his arms around my waist, hands cupping my breasts from behind. I felt the rock of his body as he moved slightly, a gap in the mold of our bodies.

"Yeah. A long time ago."

I hadn't expected an affirmative response, the words catching me off guard, the raw pain in his voice making *a long time ago* seem not that long ago at all. I wanted to roll over, wanted to see his face, but his hands tightened, nailed me back to his chest, like he could see my thoughts and wanted to block them.

Jealousy prickled through me, foreign and ugly in my veins. I knew that there had to be others, relationships before me, lives lived before we met at that casino. He wasn't a man afraid of commitment, seemed custom fit for a relationship, but he'd spoken so little about his past. I'd asked; he'd evaded. It really seemed like, prior to meeting me, he had worked and traveled, little else. But *now*, a break in his tone, a weakness revealed. He had loved someone enough *to die* for them. Had I ever loved someone that greatly? Would I one day love him that much? I could feel it coming, the possibilities behind the jump that my heart was taking, each trip, each phone conversation, each gift another chip in the wall of my heart. Soon, he'd break through, and I'd have fallen. I only had to hope, at that point, that he'd have fallen for me too. "What happened?" I whispered, struggling to keep my voice light.

"She died." He retightened his arms, gripped me closer, the dead tone of the words more scary to me than the raw shake of the prior ones. We laid there in silence, past the roll of the credits, past the intro to the next film. We laid there in silence until, at some point in the night, I fell asleep.

chapter 21

4 months before

Riley Johnson & Brett Jacobs

The words were in perfect calligraphy, the letters glimmering off the cream envelope at me. Of course Chelsea redid the envelopes. Of course she sent me a duplicate invite, one to replace the 'Riley Johnson & Guest' that she'd sent four months earlier. Pushy had always been a quick word used to describe her. She wanted Brett there, the invite one more hint just in case I didn't get the first five. It was her wedding, her big day, and, for some reason, her walking down the aisle was an act incomplete if not paired with supreme discomfort on my end.

"I'm not bringing him," I'd said, just three days earlier, our toes spread and perched upon pedicure benches, mine half-way on their way to becoming 'Barefoot in Barcelona' nude, while Chelsea went with a more appropriate 'Señorita Rose-alita' pink. "It'd be a disaster, trying to introduce him to all of Quincy at once. Plus, the focus and gossip should be on you and Jarad, not me and my weekend fling."

"Seriously, shut up. It's way past a weekend fling at this point. Stop assuming it's gonna end and start looking at this like a serious relationship. It'd be an insult to that relationship to not bring him."

She'd been right. I knew that. I was playing goalie with my heart, running around after it with a stick and whacking it into place whenever it got happy or hopeful, whacking extra hard when words like *I love you* threatened to spill out. Could a relationship survive in that environment? Could it thrive? When had I gotten so afraid of love and hope that I strangled it to death with my insecurity? Maybe it was easier to date an ugly man, one with obvious flaws, one who belched and couldn't dress, and wasn't so damn perfectly tempting. At least then I'd feel confident.

I tapped the envelope against my palm and checked out the postmark as I walked up the driveway. Three days earlier. That was what I got for not checking my mail every day. She must have left the nail salon and driven *straight* home, her fresh nails pulling out a new invite before the polish had even set.

I threw the invite, along with the rest of my mail, on the kitchen counter, fed Miller, and flipped on the bathroom light. Ran a hot bath and lit a candle. Submerged myself in bubbles and dozed a little, contemplating the idea of Brett as a wedding date.

It'd be horrible. Our bridesmaid dresses were *coral* for God's sake.

My parents would be there. As would my ex. As would all of the girls. As would my boss. As would almost every other person in Quincy.

It'd put pressure on our relationship. Didn't all weddings? I'm pretty sure I read that in *Cosmo* once. "Never Take a Man to a Wedding" ... Something like that was the title. The article had had bullet points and everything. Something about how we'd look needy, and they'd feel pressured to flee.

Plus ... this was Quincy. Not a five-star resort or a private beach home, or a steak restaurant with candles and champagne. I didn't even know if our relationship would work in the light of an average day. Brett might be some finery vampire, whose skin might eat away in the presence of polyester, rednecks, and American beer.

By the time the water was cool, my toe thumbing the drain before stepping out, my mind had all but decided. I *would*, damn the consequences, invite him. Warn him of the perils involved, and let him make his own decision. He was a big boy. And if Chelsea McCrory's wedding ended up being the demise of our relationship, then it wasn't built to last anyway.

I dried off, got in pajamas, and found my phone, seeing a new text from him, a photo. I opened up the pic while sticking popcorn in the microwave—my dinner that evening. It took my mind an extra second to process the photo, the cream invitation in his hand identical to my own, just a few feet away on my counter.

Chelsea McCrory. That little witch. She'd sent him his own invite, my name casually beside his own in that damn perfect calligraphy script.

And … just like that, I lost all credit for making my own decision to invite Brett. Just like that I had to call him and explain that I really *did* want him to come to my best friend's wedding, which was in two weeks … and I hadn't made any previous mention of.

My hands tightened on the phone, and I seriously contemplated throwing the damn thing against the wall. Instead, I took a deep breath, collected my thoughts, and called Brett.

chapter 22
Kitten

"Today's lesson is about removal of hope. The strongest slaves hold out for an idea of release, of rescue. That makes it infinitely harder for them to adjust to and enjoy life as a slave." He picked up his pen.

I will never adjust to this. I will never enjoy this.

"Do you have hope, Kitten?"

"No." *Yes.*

"Is there someone that you envision rescuing you?"

"No." *Brett.*

"I've told you about this cell. About the ten pounds of concrete that surround each of your bars. About the fact that, should you somehow escape this cell, that you will still be locked in the basement, a windowless space whose door has four deadbolts. The closest house is a half-mile away. I live alone. Your screams don't carry past this room. Your hope for escape, or for rescue, should be dead."

"It is." *Brett will save me. He will look for me. He will find me.*

"No..." He stood and walked in a small circle around me, my knees on the hard concrete, my hands on my thighs, my eyes closed. I was so tired. "I don't believe it is. I believe you still have hope, Kitten."

I didn't know what that meant - his belief in my hope - but when he pulled my chin up and I stared into his eyes, I knew that it was bad. I knew I had failed another test.

My hardest day was not the first time I was raped. Or when I spent unknown hours handcuffed in my own defecation. Or when I was whipped. My hardest day was that one, when I lost my teeth. Four of them, molars taken out with a tool that looked like expensive pliers.

And the hardest part wasn't the pain — it did exist, but he allowed me pills. The hardest part was when I was told the reason, Master stopping on his way out to deliver the news, my captured teeth in a Ziploc bag hanging from his hand. When I was told that it was for when the remains of my body were found.

"I'm sorry, Kitten. Your hope was keeping you too strong, making it too difficult. Later, you'll understand, you'll appreciate this."

I *did* actually, some time later, appreciate it. Not for the loss of hope, but that he didn't take a finger or toe to use to stage my death. The teeth hurt, but I wasn't left with any deformities or outward scars. When I tested a smile at the dusty mirror above the sink, I looked normal. As normal as a girl in a basement cell could look. A girl who had a habitual black eye and split upper lip.

After he pulled my teeth, I struggled, through the haze of medication and pain, to speak, to ask intelligent questions. But he silenced me, laying a firm hand over my sore mouth, his lips coming down to my forehead with a soft press. "It's only hard for a brief while," he whispered against my hairline. "The quicker you let go, the better it will be."

I had stilled, hating the weight of his hand, the heat of his breath, the brush of his lips. Had fallen into the role of dutiful slave, the one who pleased him, the one who limited the level of contact that was needed. I laid still, the fight going out of my features, my muscles falling limp, my questions disappearing, replaced by the simple thought that *Iwillneverletgo*. A tear leaked down my cheek when I closed my eyes, and I breathed easier when he released my mouth, his lips leaving my forehead in one wet smack, the creak of his shoes heard when he stood. I lay in place, my jaw aching, more tears streaming, and repeated the mantra.

I would never let go.

I loved Brett, and he would keep looking.
I would never let go.
I loved Brett, and he would keep...
The medication took me away.

chapter 23

"So you *do* want me to come."

I swallowed a big gulp of Mountain Dew. "Yes. But I want you to understand what you're getting into."

"I've been to weddings before. I have a tux."

"God no. *Don't* wear a tux." Yep, a definite disaster. Gargantuan.

He laughed. "Okay. You seem stressed about this."

"I am. Terrified actually."

"Then I won't go."

I took a deep breath. Jumped off the cliff. "I think you should. I will be a basket case and everything that can possibly go wrong will, but I think you should come. Really."

"I don't want you to feel forced into this."

Now I laughed. "I don't want to force *you* into it."

"Anything involving you I'll never have to be forced into. Trust me on that."

I was losing this battle, my caution not strong enough to fight the fall of my heart. "Okay."

"When should I arrive? This invitation says the wedding's next Saturday night."

"Are you working that weekend?" He seemed to work every weekend, our trips often interspersed with his meetings or functions. I didn't mind. It gave me some alone time, a chance to visit the spa or catch up on my reading. Or more recently, catch up with the girls on my new phone.

"Nothing I can't get someone else to handle."

"Then come Friday. You can stay with me." I felt suddenly shy, like the assumption of his lodging was forward – even though we'd left the separate rooms arrangement back in Aruba.

"And what about this weekend? Can I steal you for a few days? The Caribbean weather is supposed to be perfect."

I groaned. "I can't. Chelsea has us all working overtime. Saturday night we're having a sleepover at her house and assembling the favors. She'll kill me if I flake out." It was true. She *literally* would. She'd already described to me how she'd do it (strangle me with her garter belt), and where she'd put my body (in Lake Talquin, weighted down with the party favors I so carelessly skipped out on). Plus, forgetting the imminent threat of death, there was the fact that I missed my friends.

"A sleepover?"

I lost a little of my stress in the giggle at his response. "Yes, a sleepover. What, you and your friends don't have sleepovers?"

"Are hair braiding and naked pillow fights involved?"

"Oh yes," I teased, dropping my voice lower while simultaneously shaking out the popcorn into a bowl. What could I say? I was a good multitasker. Could pull off sexy seductress and gourmet dinner preparer, all at the same time. "Naked pillow fights are right before skinny dipping and whipped cream wrestling."

"Fine." He let out a troubled exhale. "It'll be a long two weeks."

I smiled. "For me too."

"So ... no tux?"

"No!" I said sharply. "Khakis and a button-up." Granted, had it been up to Chelsea's expensive Atlanta wedding planner, tuxes would have been standard. We'd had to remind her, several times over the last year, that ninety-nine percent of the attendees were country folk and not millionaires. "No tie." I added. "And even in *that*, I can't guarantee you won't be called a city boy."

"It's okay. I kinda *am* a city boy."

I smiled. And in that moment, despite everything stacked against us, I felt a glimmer of hope that we would survive the wedding weekend.

chapter 24

3 months, 2 weeks before

tight (tīt)
(adj.) barely allowing time for completion
"a tight schedule"

It was official. Brett was coming to the wedding which meant he was coming *here*, would stay in my house, touch my stuff, pet my dog. Would meet my friends again, my parents—oh god, my *father*. All because Chelsea couldn't mind her own business. I stared at my living room in a mild state of panic. I'd had two weeks to prepare; this wasn't a surprise. Had twelve days and nights to work down my carefully written "to do" list.

Twelve days. And yet, two hours before Brett landed, only three items were crossed off.

> *Get a manicure/pedicure.*
> *~~Shave.~~*
> *Wash all dirty clothes.*
> *Fold all clothes.*
> *~~Drop off dry cleaning.~~*
> *Stock the kitchen with enough food to look normal.*
> *Buy candles and burn throughout house the week before.*
> *Do baseboards.*
> *Change sheets.*

Wipe down all surfaces and toss all trash.
Hide all clutter.
Move high school awards and items to garage.
Track down and hide all Modern Bride issues.
~~*Throw away ruffled pillows and toilet seat cover.*~~
Hide   super   tampon   boxes   and   any   embarrassing
bathroom/medication items.
Kidnap Megan, Tammy, Jena, and Mitzi and lock them away
until Brett leaves.

Okay, so the last item was a joke. Sort of. A joke only because the feasibility of kidnapping four bridesmaids in such a short time frame seemed a bit ambitious for a novice criminal. But, even if I threw that item off the list, I still had a shitload of work to do in a short length of time. I moved to the bedroom, sweeping my hair into a ponytail and unbuttoning my shirt with hasty fingers. I stepped out of my skirt and moved to the dresser before retracing my steps, picking up the discarded items and putting them into the hamper.

I was sure there were normal individuals out there who *liked* cleaning ... but I hated it. Hated it *with a passion*. If there were a way to murder Cleaning in the study with a candlestick, I'd be the guilty Miss Scarlet. I normally straightened up on Sunday mornings, sometime between cereal and an afternoon nap. But my weekend excursions with Brett had pushed those Sunday cleanings off by ... four weeks? Five? I mentally added "Clean toilet" to the list. Then I changed into a T-shirt and jean shorts and got to work.

***

Two hours and forty-three minutes later, my panic had reached a more manageable level, one where exhaustion sat on its chest and made it shut the hell up. I swapped my sweaty tee for a cute tank top and grabbed my keys, giving the house a quick glance over before heading for the car.

It looked good. Clean, but not like I'd prepared for him. For once, I was grateful for such a small home, the dirt not having too much square footage in which to hide. Checking my watch, I swore at the time, grabbing my cell from the counter and running out the door.

***

"You hungry?" I tapped my fingers against the steering wheel, noting, for the first time, the cracks in its vinyl. I wondered what kind of car Brett drives. Seems weird that I didn't know that. That I hadn't been to his city, his house.

"Starving. I had some crackers on the plane, but nothing else." He relaxed in the passenger seat, his hand resting on the back of my headrest, the faint scent of soap and a light cologne drifting over with his shift into place.

My stomach growled, as if it had the right to input an opinion. The sound reminded me of my failure to eat, not since eleven this morning, when I scarfed down a Wendy's chicken salad behind the tellers. I probably burned a thousand calories during my cleaning frenzy. I was surprised my body hadn't gone into shock.

"What's a good local restaurant?"

I smiled. "Beverly's is good, just be prepared."

"For what?"

"Everything." Might as well rip off the Band-Aid now. On the upside, it *was* after eight. Maybe the dinner crowd had thinned.

***

Nope. The dinner crowd was still in full force when I pulled into the gravel lot. My eyes scanned and recognized at least ten of the trucks in the lot. I felt a pit form in my cavernously empty stomach.

"Lots of trucks," Brett commented.

"Farming is a major industry here. Add that to the redneck factor, and you've got testosterone fighting via mud flaps at every four-way." I put the car into park and leaned forward. Kissed him lightly on the lips. "Thank you for coming here."

"Thank you for letting me."

"It's been nice knowing you." I grinned wryly.

"It won't be that bad, I promise."

I kissed his naïve little mouth and turned off the car.

chapter 25

Beverly's was one big room, a buffet set on the back wall, picnic tables filling the large, paisley-wallpapered space. There were no private tables; everyone grabbed any available seat, community pitchers of tea on the tables, refilled on a regular basis by one of Beverly's four girls. There was no menu, and there weren't any specials. Lunch was seven bucks, dinner was ten, and credit cards weren't accepted. Sweet tea, coffee, and water were the only drink options, and you cleared your own plate when done. When short on cash, Beverly had an IOU form at the front counter that you could complete and settle up when times got better.

I grabbed Brett's hand and sucked in, squeezing between two tables and heading deeper into the room, beelining for an open spot at Table 9. I smiled at the Rutledges and Corina Rose, mouthed a "hey" to Patty Thomas. Breathed a sigh of relief when I stepped into the bench, flashing smiles to the individuals on either side. Watched Brett as he made his way to the other side. He wore a T-shirt and jeans with tennis shoes. I had told him to dress casual, had been worried that he'd stick out. But even in that, he looked expensive, couldn't hide the aura of confidence and wealth that separated him from every other man in this room.

"This place is nice."

I didn't know if Brett was just being polite, but, in our town, it was the best food you were gonna find. I met his eyes and was pleased to see sincerity in them. I shrugged. "The food's really good."

"Do we have a waitress?"

I laughed. "Sorta. Beverly'll come by with plates and glasses. It's her way of greeting everyone. Anything you need, that'll be the only time we see her, so be sure to ask for it then."

He eyed the row of condiments lining the table's middle. "I'll be fine."

"Good. She doesn't like extra work."

"Are you talking about me, missy?" Beverly's voice craned through the air and smacked me on the back of my head. I gave Brett a look of mock panic and turned around, accepting the woman's fierce hug, her long nails digging into me like it'd been weeks instead of days.

"All good things," I reassured.

"Humph. Likely. Who's this?" She eyed Brett like he was a piece of choice fried chicken. "This the rich South Florida man you've been running off with?"

Brett's eyebrows rose at the comment, the dimple in his cheek exposed when he stood and offered his hand across the table. "Brett Jacobs," he said smoothly. "While I *am* from South Florida, I can't vouch for the rest of the description."

I made a face at him before recovering, smiling at Beverly. "Yes, Brett is my new boyfriend. He's visiting this weekend from Fort Lauderdale."

"Oooh ... Fort Lauderdale!" Beverly waved her palms from side to side like a can-can routine. "Fancy! And you'll be here all weekend?"

"Yes." Brett smiled and I cringed at his omission of 'ma'am.' The word was a Southern requirement, a verbal side dish that must accompany every course. It didn't matter if the person addressed was six years old. Or twenty. Or ninety. In the South, we said 'please' and 'thank you,' 'sir,' and 'ma'am.' I saw Beverly's eyes flick to me. She stiffly held out two plates, stacking a couple of silverware rolls on top of them. I took the plates, Brett's hands reaching out for the glasses.

"The dessert today is lemon pie," Beverly said pointedly, as if there was a code word stuck somewhere in that sentence.

"Yum." I set the silverware down. "Thanks Beverly."

***

"What did I do wrong?" Brett spoke from the side of his mouth as he heaped an impressive amount of mashed potatoes on his plate. Our elbows knocked each other, a woman on my right crowding me in her haste for fried catfish.

"What do you mean?" I pointed to the gravy ladle, and he passed it over.

"The look that passed between you two. I did something wrong."

"Oh." I smiled. "You didn't say 'ma'am' when you responded to her."

He paused, the sudden halt messing up the flow of the line. I bumped him with my hip and nodded at him to continue. "What ... a Southern faux pas?" he asked.

"Yes. *Sir*." I added the second word, grinning at him. "See how easy it is?"

He leaned over, pressing a kiss on my cheek, before pausing at my ear. "I love you." On his way back to standing, my cheeks burning red from the confession, he dipped back down. "Ma'am," he added, gently pinching my butt.

Wait—what? "Now you got it." I mumbled, grabbed a roll and looked up at him, his eyes skimming the buffet one last time. I didn't even know how to respond, didn't expect the buffet line at Beverly's to be the place where *this* moment would happen. But Brett didn't seem to need a response, his legs already in motion, his broad shoulders moving through the tables.

I followed him back to the table and wished I had chosen a less public venue.

***

Brett's fork was scraping his plate when the cops showed up. A foursome, swaggering through the front door, shaking hands and greeting citizens on their way to our table. They surrounded us, John

Bingham placing a friendly hand on my shoulder as he leaned over and brushed his lips over my cheek. Brett's eyes watched the movement, his face tightening slightly as he set down his fork. I scooted back, my eyes sweeping over the foursome, identical in their green uniforms, all wearing a relaxed expression of arrogance and control.

Blake Gadsden: Married Marianna Nichols last March, I was a bridesmaid, along with *eighteen* other emerald-ensconced beauties.

Russell Shaverton: Our high school quarterback. 3 brain cells. 100 good intentions.

Clive Summerbell: Last month, I opened a savings account for him. He once cheated on Janice Weiland but nobody talks about that.

And … finally … the man whose hand still rested on my shoulder. John Bingham: My high school sweetheart. The man I lost my virginity to fourteen years ago. Prom king. Once proposed marriage in a field by his grandfather's pond with a tiny solitaire. I said no; it didn't go over well. My father still hasn't recovered.

I smiled, tilting my head back and narrowing my eyes up at John. "John. What are you boys doing here? Shouldn't you be keeping the streets safe?"

"Already handled." He flashed a smile back, the fingers of his hand moving slightly, a caress against the skin of my shoulder.

Brett's eyes met mine as he stood, the group of men stepping back slightly as the air became more crowded. "I'm sorry, I haven't had the pleasure of meeting you. Brett Jacobs." He held out his hand, my shoulder spared for a brief moment as John reached across, my eyes watching their hands meet.

"Brett, this is John, Russell, Hank, and Blake." I zipped around the circle. "Boys, this is my boyfriend, Brett. He's in town for Chelsea's wedding."

"Is that so?" John put his hand on the table, lifting his leg through as if he was going to sit down.

I smacked his leg, stopping the moment. "We're having dinner, John. Give us some privacy."

"I'm just being friendly, Ril." He dipped his head toward me, and I scowled in response.

"I know friendly. Ya'll git. I heard someone's stealing DVDs from Rick's. Go investigate."

"All those trips to Tahiti got you outta the loop. We snagged Sharon Marzola for that last week. Caught her red-handed via stakeout." He winked proudly at me, like I should be impressed. "You done eating?" he nodded at Brett.

"Yes." Brett's mouth twitched as he glanced at me, and I laughed, well aware that he—damn the social consequences—would not be addressing John as 'sir.'

"Russell, show the visitor some Quincy hospitality." John nodded to the plate, and I reached out, stopping the skinny arm before it escaped with Brett's dirty plate and silverware.

"We got it. John, stop it." I stood, suddenly too close to him, and folded my arms.

"I'm just following orders, princess."

My eyes literally rolled themselves. "I'll take it up with the chief."

"If that's what you want." He shrugged, shaking his head briefly at Russell, whose hand dropped underneath mine.

"It was nice to meet you guys." Brett settled back down, dragging his plate closer.

"Thanks for stopping by. I'm sure we'll see you all tomorrow." I glared at John and slid back onto the bench.

"I'm sorry about that." I said the words softly, as soon as the glass door clanged shut behind the foursome.

He laughed, ripping a piece of bread in two and dipping it in the butter. "Don't. It was entertaining. I take it you have a history with the blond?"

"Yeah. High school sweethearts."

"He single?"

"Yes."

"Should I be worried?" He set down the bread.

I smiled. "No. But go easy on him. He hasn't had to see me with anyone for a while. It's ... strange for him. Hearing the stories and now, seeing you here."

"What are the stories?"

"Oh, you know. Dark, handsome stranger whisking off innocent, sweet, loved-by-all Riley Johnson. Corrupting her weekends before sending her back a ruined woman."

"Oh, is *that* what they're saying?" His mouth curved.

I nodded, widening my eyes. "Oh yes. It's quite the scandal."

"Loved by all?" His skeptical look made me laugh.

"Loved by *most*," I conceded. *Crap.* We were back in the *love* territory, and I swear it was by accident. My heart picked up, a knot suddenly tight in my abdomen.

"What was all the fighting over my plate? Is that some kind of hazing ritual here in the South? Clearing someone else's dirty dishes?" I loved the way his eyes smiled. I felt like they didn't do that when we met.

"Oh. They wanted your prints and DNA."

The eye smile thing he'd had working stopped. "For dating you?"

I played with the fork in my mouth, testing the strength of it with my teeth before releasing it. "Yep."

"Isn't that a violation of some cop law—can't they be fired for that?" He was pissed, and I raised my eyebrows at him.

"I stopped it, Brett. Besides, I'm not certain it was all John's doing. My father is probably behind it."

"Your father? What does he have to do with them?"

"He's their boss. Quincy's Chief of Police."

I'd never really *seen* the reaction to my father's job before. Not from a prospective love interest. And I didn't know if I hadn't seen a reaction because they didn't exist, or because the reaction was diluted through a phone call or word of mouth. But there, in Beverly's restaurant, Brett recoiled. Physically retreated away from me as if I was contaminated.

"What?" I leaned forward, unwilling to let him separate us. "It's not that big of a deal."

"It just seems like something you would have mentioned."

"Why? I haven't told you my mother works as a pharmacy tech. Will that also cause you to break that bench in your haste to escape?"

He leaned forward once again. "Don't be ridiculous. I was just surprised."

"Why?"

"I don't know. You've never mentioned your parents."

"Neither have you. And you haven't asked," I pointed out.

He ran a hand through his hair, glancing to the right, his eyes meeting with Dorothy Riepenhoff, who raised her eyebrows at him as if waiting for his response. He glanced from her to me, his eyes imperceptibly squinting as if to question her invasion. I hid a smile behind a gulp of tea. *He* was the one who wanted to visit Quincy.

"Plus, you love me. So you can't really run now," I offered, watching his eyes flip to mine. There. I brought it up. Before we even left the restaurant. Pretty good for a girl who'd recently accused herself of being afraid of commitment.

His mouth twitched. "What a sad soul I'd make, hopelessly lost in unrequited love, tied to a girl with a police chief father."

I tilted my head and took another sip, hiding behind the clouded glass. "It may be reciprocated," I mumbled.

"What's that?" His hand gently pushed the glass away.

"Maybe. Maybe I do have feelings for you."

"Maybe," he repeated. "Maybe you love me?"

"Yes. Kinda."

"You can't kinda love someone."

"No?" I returned the glass to my mouth for a conversation-stalling sip.

"No. I won't allow it." He stood, placing both hands on the table and leaned forward, across the space. Next to him, Dorothy stared at us and clapped excitedly like she was about to win something. "Say it,

Riley Johnson, and I'll march down to the precinct right now and let your dad take a pint of my blood."

I stood and leaned forward, our mouths whispers away from each other. "Bold words, Mr. Jacobs."

"I got a whole town of men to fight through." He grinned. "Say it and let me kiss you."

Love. Was I ready to say it? How could I not? Wasn't love what I had been feeling? The breathless high, the tug at my heart, the obsessive want for more of him, all the time, as much as I could get? Wasn't love the yearn I felt when our phone calls ended, the need I felt as soon as he touched me, the crack of my barriers every time he smiled?

It was, it had to be, and I didn't stop the words; they flowed like blood, scary and exhilarating all at the same time. "I love you."

Then, there, in Beverly's diner, he grabbed the back of my head, claimed my mouth with his kiss, and the restaurant erupted in cheers.

It was a Hollywood moment, one that would make its way down every dirt road in Quincy that night.

chapter 26

We didn't go to the precinct. For one, it was nine on a Friday night. Dad was at home, his feet already up in the recliner, Mom in her pajamas and rollers. For two, it'd be the most unromantic follow-up to a confession of love in the History of Great Love Stories and Brett's comment had been, for the most part, made in jest. For three, Brett's mouth was on my neck, his hand up my shirt, my ass shifting against the car seat as I fought to keep my hands on the wheel. "Brett, let me focus. I'm gonna drive off into the ditch."

"Would that be so bad? Ditches sound like an excuse to bend you over this hood." He pulled at the straps of my tank top, and I squirmed when my breasts were exposed.

"Trust me, it'll lose all sex appeal when we have to call one of my exes to pull us out. That'll put a hole in your ego."

He groaned, sitting back in his seat, his hand instead gripping my thigh, his thumb brushing against the denim. "Good point. How *many* exes do you have in this town?"

I squinted, ticking back through the years. "Well ... I was a hot little ticket in elementary school."

"I knew it. A loose woman." He clicked his tongue. "I don't blame them all for still being crazy about you. If something happens to us, feel free to call me if you're ever broke down in South Florida. I'll puff out my chest and drop everything to come to your rescue. And I'll do my best to steal you from whoever's heart you happen to—at that point in time—hold."

"That's so..." I tilted my head. "Sweet? Creepy? Depressing?"

He laughed. "Sweet. Romantic. Chivalrous."

"Hmmm." I slowed, a blinker unnecessary, no souls for miles, and turned down my driveway.

"This is you?" Brett glanced out the window at the house, the front porch light on, the fields around it dark in the night.

"Yep. Home sweet home."

"Pretty desolate."

"It's the country. Everything's desolate. I'm only three miles from town."

"You own it?"

"Not really. It's my grandma's—was one of their worker's homes, back when they farmed. I'm sure I'll inherit it, but for now, I've got it as long as I want it. I pay the taxes and repairs on it."

I pulled to a stop, the headlights shining on the front porch, one that sloped a little to the right, the rusted tin roof giving it an extra layer of character. Brett leaned forward. "Repairs are gonna include a new roof pretty soon."

"Oooh ... a boat salesman *and* a roof expert. Looks like I hit the jackpot." I undid my seatbelt and popped open the door.

Throwing my purse over a shoulder, I grinned at Miller, who had ducked out the doggie door and stood, all four feet flat on the porch, his head low, shoulders hunched, teeth bared. An intimidating protector, as long as the trespasser didn't have a Milk-Bone in hand.

"Easy Miller." I moved past Brett. "Wait a second." I walked up the stairs, crouching next to the black lab, his posture unchanging. Rubbing his back and ears, I cooed to him while beckoning Brett closer. "It's okay, Miller. Brett is friendly. We love friends, don't we?" Underneath my hands, his muscles relaxed, his vigilance broken with a giant lick in my direction, the tongue catching me square on the lips. I laughed, wiping my mouth with my forearm and shoving at the dog.

"Am I safe?" Brett asked, coming to a stop at the bottom of the steps.

"You're safe. Just come say hi so he knows you're a good guy."

Brett climbed the steps and crouched beside me, Miller giving him a tentative sniff before leaning into his scratch, one big paw lifting and resting on Brett's knee. "That's it?" He chuckled. "I'm in?"

"You're in. Bring him a bone tomorrow and he'll be committed for life."

I stood, brushing off the dog hair and headed to the door, Brett's hand on my elbow when I opened it. "You don't lock it?"

"You've lived in a big city too long. We all know each other here. And Miller guards the place. If something was up, he'd tell me."

He frowned at me, his hand still on my elbow, his eyes sweeping over the dark fields before returning to my face. "Lock up. For me. I won't be able to sleep another night in Lauderdale knowing you're coming home to an unlocked house."

I elbowed loose. "Fine. I'll lock up. I don't even know where the damn keys are, but I'll lock up. Happy?"

"Hardly."

I bit back a response, shutting the door, the one with the giant doggie door on it, one that a man of any size could crawl through. He wanted the door to be locked? Whatever. I set my purse on the counter and flipped on the lamp.

"Voila. The kitchen."

He ran a hand over the Formica surface, leaning forward and testing the strength of the structure, sending me a flirtatious smile.

"Keep smiling. That's about the only thing that surface is good for."

He reached out, winding a finger through the belt loops of my jeans and dragging me over to the sink, his body trapping me against the counter. "Does that mean you've tried it out?" His nose ran down my neck as he growled against the cords of my throat.

"It means I don't cook. I'm a failure to Southern women everywhere."

He hooked his hands underneath the back of my thighs, lifting me up and setting me on the counter, my shriek of surprise suppressing when he looked up at me.

Damn. The man was beautiful; I knew that from the first time I saw him. But this was a new view, one I hadn't seen. His chin up, eyes on fire with lust and possession and love. He fisted the bottom of my shirt and tugged it up and over my head, his eyes recapturing mine the minute the black tank was gone. "I always thought cooking was a poor use for a kitchen anyway."

"Really?" I breathed, my eyes dropping when his hands settled on my breasts. I was glad I changed into lace, the last-minute swap now making this moment so much hotter and more accessible than my sweaty sports bra would have allowed.

"Oh yeah. Especially when the kitchen is owned by a woman like you."

"You mean one who can't cook?" My bra straps were now hanging off my shoulders, his right hand sliding around my back and tugging at the clasp.

"No. I mean one who should be kissed at every opportunity."

"Just kissed?" I moaned when my bra dropped free and his mouth lowered, down the curve of my cleavage, his hands offering up my breasts, gently caressing the flesh as if it was sacred.

"Kissed. Worshipped. Seduced. Fucked within an inch of her life."

"In that case, Mr. Jacobs, the bedroom is behind you," I whispered.

"Is that an invitation?"

"It's an order."

"Yes, ma'am." He wrapped his hands around my waist, fireman carrying me through the living room, hitting the bathroom door by accident, then kicking open the bedroom door and carrying me through. The last thing I saw, before falling onto the bed, was Miller's curious face, the door swinging shut on his chocolate brown snout.

chapter 27
Kitten

Back when I was free, I was a reader. I never read sex slave books, but I was aware of the market, had scrolled past the bestselling titles on my Kindle as I searched for my vanilla romances. I knew, from my brief perusals, that the sex slave relationship was often romanticized, the Master an ultimate alpha male, one who ordered fabulous sex while creating a deeper bond with the captive. While those accounts were fiction, I did understand that there was a psychological break that occurred when a woman was kept like an animal, dependent on one individual for her basic human needs.

Now, in this concrete basement, my knowledge of such relationships had grown one-thousandfold. In part, because of my actual experience. But more so, because of his word vomit. The man had approached our relationship like a science, meticulously testing different practices and recording it in his binders. I didn't know if he was training for the Slave Olympics or researching for a book, but his questions, his speeches, his explanations had taught me far more about the psychology than I ever wanted to know. I would never tell him, but a small part of me understood Stockholm syndrome. I had felt tugs of loneliness, surges of pride, bits of desire for approval. The breaks had come when I was at my weakest, their arrival giving me a peek into the rabbit hole that always existed in these walls, the ever-present risk to connect out of sheer necessity with my captor.

But that would not be my story. I didn't have to, in the bones of my soul, be strong. That was what my memories were for. To ground me, to be my lifeline.

"God, you're incredible," Brett rolled me onto my back, his body above mine, his chest wet with sweat, my own breasts heaving from the exertion of our activities. Above him, the pattern of my bedroom ceiling, pale yellow painted boards that shimmered in the afternoon sun.

"You say that every time," I chided, smiling up at him.

"I can't help it. I'm a man who speaks the truth, it's my curse." He bent forward, his mouth soft on mine before he moved to my jaw, then my neck. I felt his neck move, pushing my legs apart, and I wrapped them around his waist. "No," he pushed at my thighs, keeping them open, his body sliding down mine, the trail of his mouth leaving a teasing line across my breasts, stomach, and hip. He stopped at my open legs, a hand reverently passing over me, my back arching into his touch, the hot exhale of his breath tickling me before he lowered his mouth. I closed my eyes and couldn't stop the curse when it ripped through me at the first contact of his tongue.

One day, I would be out of here. One day, we would be reunited.

That was the day I lived for, fought for.

chapter 28

I was a Daddy's girl, always had been. My connection was stronger with him than my mother. I didn't know why, except to say that my mother—for some reason or another—had wanted a boy. A strange thing, especially in the South. Especially from a woman who epitomized femininity, from her painted red toes to the rollers she wore to bed at night. But a boy was what she always wanted and when I'd turned up, my father was the one who'd welcomed me with unconditional love.

So yes, we were close. He was protective. And his position as Chief of Police, a position he'd held for the last twenty-two years, had often been used to his advantage as a father.

There was the time when John and I were screwing, knee-deep in Israel Duran's barn straw, and two black and whites pulled in, lights blazing. I had been sixteen and skipping school. They'd put the both of us in the back of the squad car and marched us into my father's office. That night, a flashlight in mouth—I found a tracking device underneath the rear bumper of my Sunfire.

There was the time when I was arrested at UGA, along with fourteen others, victims of a house-party raid. A room full of underage drinking, weed, and pills on the dining room table, and we were all brought in and kept overnight. I made the mistake of using my one phone call to call my father. Thought that Daddy Dearest might use some political sway to get me released before daybreak. A stupid, drunk decision. I sobbed into the phone, told him I hadn't been doing drugs, and that I'd only had one Bud Light. Thirty minutes later, I'd had a rape exam, full drug panel working on my blood, and had blown a .21 on a Breathalyzer. They reported the findings (marijuana in my system, no rape, but signs of recent sexual activity) to my father, and I spent two nights in an Athens jail cell, twice what any of my friends endured. And trust me, those extra twenty-four hours sucked.

There had been very few moments where I'd appreciated my father's position. The encounter with the boys at Beverly's Diner smelled of his involvement. I'd have to pull him aside at the wedding. Make it clear that he needed to keep his distance. Respect my privacy and new relationship. Allow me to live my own life. I wasn't sixteen anymore. I could make my own decisions and mistakes. I sipped Folgers and wondered how Dad would react, both to my mandate and to meeting Brett. Mom would be easy. Any person who increased her likelihood of grandchildren (maybe this time it'd be a boy!) would be embraced.

"So." Brett wandered in, pulling a shirt over his head, the stretch and pop of abs causing my eyes to linger. "What's the plan for today?"

I lifted my head from the cup. "Not sure. I was just mulling over that. We need to be at the church at three. Until then, it's pretty open."

"You always have such a serious expression when musing over lunch plans?"

I smiled and took another sip, letting the bitter heat warm my throat. "I was thinking about my parents. Not sure if they'll scare you off tonight."

"These are the police chief/pharmacy tech parents?" Brett asked, picking up an apple from the bowl and asking permission with his eyes. I waved him on, lifting my feet from the other dining room chair and kicking it out for him.

"Yes. The only ones I got."

He shrugged. "Some people have two."

"Do you?"

He chewed a bite of apple, the act taking a minute, his Adam's apple bulging as he swallowed. "Nope. Just one. My parents are still married."

"Look at us. Two surviving children in a sea of broken families."

"A good omen for the future of our marriage." He looked up, winked.

"Easy, Fabio." I sipped my coffee. "One relationship milestone at a time."

"I didn't mean to pressure you last night. With the 'I love you' stuff."

"I wouldn't have said it back if I didn't mean it." I reached out, requesting the apple, and he passed it over, letting me steal a bite. "Let me get dressed. We can run into town and I'll buy you a real breakfast, give you the five dollar tour."

He caught me as I passed, his hand gently on my waist as he pushed me against the wall and stole a kiss. "I do love you, Miss Johnson."

I rose to my tippy toes and kissed him back.

CHAPTER 29
BRETT

I used to be a man who didn't care. Who smiled freely, put his shoes up on the table, drank to excess, loved without reserve. Then, the woman I loved more than anything in the world was taken. That day put a cloud over my life. Changed the man I was to the man I am now. A man who considers every action. Who hides more than he gives. Who lies more than he tells the truth.

I was lying when I met Riley. Playing a part that I'd cultivated to such a point that it felt natural. I was in a role, so I kept playing it. Provided a card that contained rows of lies. Talked and hinted of a life I didn't keep. I played the part, I fucked the girl, and somehow, amid the skin and the touches and the gorgeous crook of her smile, I felt it. Felt a tugging on a part of my heart that I thought had died.

When I first met her, I should've let her go. Let her get on that jet and fly back home. Let my heart turn back to black, crush the weakness that had threatened. But I didn't. I allowed the weakness to fester, to rot at the bones of my ribcage until my chest was cracked wide open and she had crawled inside and feasted on my heart. Inhaled it until there was no longer her and I but only us.

I didn't know how to go back. Didn't know how to break off this piece of my soul and give her back. Didn't know how to sift through the lies and tell her the truth. Didn't know how to be the man she deserved without losing sight of my goal.

I didn't know how to hold on to that goal without letting it consume my future.

chapter 30

Chelsea's wedding narrowed the list of single girls down to two: Megan Gallt and myself. Megan was more in love with Jesus than any man, and would probably be single at least another five years, the pool of men in Quincy too sinful for her tastes. Me ... I hadn't really thought about marriage, not with any of my exes. Not until Brett. But being at a wedding sort of forced your brain in that direction, shoved hopes and dreams down your throat until the moment when you confronted all of it and allowed *what if.*

What if we got married? We'd have to move to Fort Lauderdale. His job was there, and it was a much bigger job than mine. I didn't mind moving. Had thought about it before I even met Brett, my restlessness in Quincy finding new ways to emerge: in my snap at a customer, my binge on Netflix series, my scan of big city job search engines late at night. I would happily move. Settle in South Florida, get a new job, find new friends, and we'd jet set back to Quincy a few weeks every year to see my friends and family. Maybe we could have an annual girls' trip to Atlantis, could relive our bachelorette party weekend.

What if we had kids? Brett would make a great dad. And I'd always wanted a child; my maternal urges sated by the fact that I had become "Aunt Riley" to Tammy, Jena, *and* Mitzi's kids. What would it be like to wake up to the sound of a child's giggle and know *we* had created that? What was this love that "changed you" and how would it feel to love a baby that much?

What if we grew old together? What if this was it, he was my soulmate and this breathless, nervous excitement that I felt whenever he reached for me, smiled at me – what if it never faded and was there forever? What if our kids had kids, and we retired together and bought vacation homes and went on cruises and played shuffleboard? What if my hair turned white, and he still loved me, and we died like that old couple in *Titanic*, our hands clasped, us entering heaven within minutes of each other?

What ifs were dangerous. *What ifs* were terrifying. I watched Brett smile at my mother and stand, reaching for her hand, and she blushed, following him to the dance floor where he carefully spun her around.

What if he broke my heart?

chapter 31

"Want to grab a movie?" I gestured to the brick storefront of Rick's Movie Rentals. "We could grill burgers and stay in tonight."

"Sure." Brett glanced out the window. "I didn't think those existed anymore."

I smiled, pulling into the gravel lot. "Watch what you say in public. We're a no-Redbox town in support of Rick."

"Really? That written down in the city code?"

I scowled at him. "Might as well be. Walmart stuck one out front—had to replace it three times due to vandalism. They finally gave up after the last one caught fire."

"Did they catch who did it?"

I laughed. "No, and no one tried. That Redbox would have meant the death of one of our town's oldest establishments. Plus," I elbowed him, "if you give Rick the secret word, he'll let you in the back where the dirty videos are." I turned off the car, leaving the keys in the ignition, and opened the door.

"Sounds clandestine."

"Oh, it is." I leaned against the front door, the chime of bells causing the round man behind the counter to look up with a smile.

"Hey Riley. It's been a while."

"Hey Rick. This is Brett—he's visiting from Lauderdale."

"Oh, I've heard." The man eased off the stool and stood, reaching a hand across the glass counter. "Nice to meet you. Take good care of our girl, you hear?"

"I'm trying." Brett smiled.

"Got anything new, Rick?" I called, dipping down the aisle.

"New ones are on the end caps."

We finally—taking our time, nothing left of the town to see—decided on *Die Hard*, grabbing some candy and microwave popcorn packets off Rick's shelf. Brett paid and we returned to the car, cracking open a box of chocolate peanuts for the ride home. I had just pulled out when Brett chuckled from the passenger seat, turning the DVD case over in his hand.

"What?"

"I was just thinking about our first dinner in Aruba. When you asked me to name a movie with singing in it." He held up the case. "Doesn't Bruce Willis sing in this? Some Christmas song while he's running around?"

I tilted my head, thinking. "I think you're right. Another shining example of your poor answering ability."

"Oh, I don't know. I think Jerry Maguire endeared you a little to me. Cracked my tough guy exterior."

"Tough guy exterior?" I laughed. "Please."

It was odd, being in my normal environment with him beside me. The two of us—out of luxury, no palm trees or ocean waves in the background. My air conditioner blew hot, our burgers got slightly burnt, and the DVD skipped every time things got interesting, but the night was a success.

That night, his body curled around mine, Miller's body warm on my feet, I fought off sleep. I just wasn't ready for the day to end and him to fly away in the morning. I had been so nervous about the weekend, the wedding, and all for nothing. Brett had been perfect, complimenting the girls, dancing most of the night on the floor, jumping onstage with the band at one moment and showcasing an impressive ability to—of all things—play the guitar. I'd fallen deeper in love with him at every turn, with every introduction, with each wink he gave me and kiss he stole. It was as if his profession of love had opened a floodgate in my heart, and my body was finally allowing a hundred powerful emotions to pour forth and link my soul to his. I had pulled aside my father early, his gruff exterior becoming even more rigid when I ordered him off of Brett.

"It's my job as your father to protect you. You'll understand it when you have a child."

"I won't ever get to that point if you scare off any potential suitors," I had said pointedly, my hand gripping his shoulder. I'd looked up at him and begged with my eyes. "Please, Daddy. Just let me have this one relationship and trust me that I know what I'm doing. Please."

His eyes had softened and he'd pulled me close to his chest. "You know I love you, Riley."

"I know, Daddy. Now prove it by trusting me." I spoke into his shirt, his hand pausing in its pat of my back.

"If that's really what you want, pumpkin."

I pulled back and beamed up at him. "Thanks, Daddy."

"Now, where is this man? At least let me give him a warning glare."

I had laughed, looping my arm through his and leading him to Brett. Dad had postured, straightening to his full height and gripping Brett's hand with a strength that had to hurt. Brett had smiled, easy and confident, his eyes direct on my father's, soft on my mother's, his head tilting when he listened to her speak. He was, simply put, perfect. And they didn't fight it, Mom beaming at me, Dad actually clapping Brett on the back near the end of the night, his mouth curving into a rare smile. If I could replay the evening a hundred times, I would. Especially our last dance, the music slow, our bodies close, his hand stealing into my hair and tugging at the pins there. I hadn't protested, I'd just rested my forehead on his as I felt the fall of curls on my bare back. "I feel like I've waited my whole life for you," he'd murmured. I'd said nothing, just released a soft sigh and taken his kiss when it'd come.

I feel like I've waited my whole life for you.
The best sentence in the world.

CHAPTER 32
BRETT

"You know that she's dead." Nicole kicked off her shoes and leaned back in the chair, bringing her feet up and sitting Indian-style.

I flinched. "I thought therapists were supposed to be gentle."

"Therapists may be. I was probably gentle with you two years ago. But I'm a psychiatrist now. And that gives me the ability to do what needs to be done."

"And to overcharge me," I grumbled, loosening my tie and pulling it off.

She laughed in response, catching the tie when I threw it at her. "I work for practically free. I get my payment in other ways."

"You're a godsend." I lowered myself into the chair across from her.

"No, but you were." Nicole straightened, picking up a stress ball, and spun slightly in the chair. "Back to Elyse." Her voice had flipped, business-like once again, and I wondered, for a moment, what her other patients saw. Was it the light-hearted tease? The serious doctor? Or did they see what I did, an infectious blend of the two?

I closed my eyes. "Back to Elyse." It always came back to Elyse. It couldn't not. Not when so much of my daily life revolved around, or was because of, her. She had touched me in life and stolen me in death. Stolen me, pulled me into this madness and wouldn't let me leave. I wasn't even sure I wanted to leave. Not when we were changing so many lives.

"I feel like you are letting Elyse jeopardize your current relationship."

"I paid for your grad school for that?" I joked, opening my eyes and lifting my head.

"You need to tell Riley."

I shook my head. "It's too dangerous. I can't bring her on the trips if she knows. If she said something wrong, gave it away—I've worked too hard on my cover." And I had. A pile of money spent burying any trace of Elyse on the Internet. False documents, backgrounds, and paper trails in place. If someone researched Brett Jacobs, they found me. If someone investigated Brett Betschart, they found next to nothing. Certainly nothing about Elyse. Certainly nothing that would link the two identities.

"Think on it." She pressed.

"I have."

She held firm, holding eye contact, and, for a brief moment, I realized how proud I was of her. An egotistic thought. "You are allowed to be happy, Brett," she said quietly. "You can let that happen."

"I know that."

I did know that. But it still felt wrong.

chapter 33

3 months before
CARIBBEAN SEA

I stretched out, my red toenails peeking at me as I propped my feet on the deck railing, the cushion beneath me warm against my wet skin. Around us, navy blue water as far as the eye could see.

"Happy?" I felt his hand tug through my hair before he played with the strands. I looked up to see Brett looking down, a smile on his face.

"How could I not be?" I patted the cushion beside me. "Come lay down."

"Sunbathing isn't my thing. I don't like to turn on all the seagulls."

I laughed, rolling over and running my hand down his stomach, his abs hard beneath his T-shirt. "Then ... why don't you turn me on instead?"

He squatted, bringing his face level with mine, and leaned in, pressing his lips to mine, his hands running up my arms and to my neck, my bathing suit top undone and stolen before my mind had a chance to catch up. He stood, smiling down at me, my hands tight to my chest as I lay on my stomach and glowered at him. "Give that back," I hissed.

"You're missing the benefits of yacht ownership. We are fifty miles from anyone ... just you and I on the boat."

"So?" I looked around furtively.

"So..." He pulled off his glasses, then the T-shirt, his hands quick as he unbuckled, unzipped, then ditched his shorts, his body completely exposed. "So, I want to fuck you in the sunshine."

He stepped closer, leaning over me, his cock pressing into my shoulder as I felt his fingers pull at the strings of my bikini bottom, the material falling away as he rolled my reluctant form over, my hands rising to cover myself, his touch gentle as they pushed my hands away, proof of his attraction growing thicker and stiffer before my eyes. "You are the most beautiful thing I have ever seen." He leaned over, crawling onto the cushion and on top of me.

"You say that to all of the girls," I scoffed, running my hands down his chest, his cock bare as it bobbed between us.

"I've never said that to anyone." He parted my legs, wrapping them around his waist, his eyes on mine when he cupped his hand over me, his thumb against my clit as he pressed his fingers inside, his other hand fisting his cock. I moaned, arching my back and pulling at his neck, wanting him closer, wanting him everywhere.

"Let me get a condom," he whispered.

"Not yet," I begged. I squeezed with my legs, ground against his hard cock, and watched his eyes darken with need, his hand moving faster, his fingers inside me quicker, the soft pant of his breath the most erotic thing I had ever heard. I ran my hand through his hair, and he bit my neck. I lost my breath in the start of an orgasm and finished with his groan in my hair. I felt his control break and loved that power belonging to me.

CHAPTER 34
BRETT

The first girl I'd ever saved was Marcia. She was a tiny brunette who was on heroin when Joel and Chris brought her in. I'd stood in the kitchen of a Bahamian rental and looked at the girl before me, her jaw working, her eyes dull and vacant, ribs showing, and felt my chest tighten. Wanted a Xanax. Wanted to walk out of that kitchen and never see another woman ever again. That life was not one I'd known. I knew butlers and Italian marble floors. I knew lobster in Tahiti and Miami Heat skyboxes with my name on the door. I hadn't known what to do with a strung-out girl who had spent the last sliver of her life servicing the needs of animals.

I had chewed at my bottom lip as I leaned against the edge of the fridge and stared at the girl. "How much did you pay for her?"

"Three thousand."

I'd closed my eyes at the sum. Wondered, in the moment before I opened them, how much her parents would have been willing to pay. Her boyfriend. Her husband. I would have paid a hundred million for Elyse. I'd wondered, as my gaze found the girl again, her teeth chattering in the quiet room, how much Elyse sold for, how much the man who'd killed her had paid for the right.

"Buy as many as you can."

chapter 35

6 weeks before

My first visit to Fort Lauderdale began in the middle of a storm, Brett's plane circling the perimeter of the city for ninety minutes before our gas levels forced us to touch down. I closed the window shades, gripped the armrests for dear life, and gave a sermon-worthy prayer in the four minutes it took us to descend.

When the wheels touched down, it was rough, the plane slamming onto the runway, my shoulders jerking forward as if I'd been yanked. I didn't care. We had landed, I was alive, and I wanted to get off that freaking plane as fast as humanly possible.

When the door opened, he was there, wetness plastered to his face, rain pelting down, his arms gathering me into his soaked chest, his mouth desperate against my cheek, my neck, my mouth. "God, I was worried," he ground out, stepping back and helping me down the steps, my magazine held over my head doing a piss-poor job of protecting me from the rain. When I hit the ground we ran, through the heavy rain, toward the hangar.

I was laughing at the sheer ridiculousness of it all, my blouse plastered to me from his wet embrace, our run through the rain pointless, the downpour one of the soak-your-bones variety. I hiccupped, a slight chill passing through me in the form of a shudder. Brett noticed, pressing a button on the side of the wall, the hangar door sliding shut. I looked around, the large, empty space big enough to hold my house. "Doesn't the plane need to come in?"

"It can wait." He pulled me closer, dragging us both down the side of the space until we reached the small kitchen. His hand was quick and efficient as he popped the front button on my jeans, my purse falling from my hand as he unzipped my pants and squatted, peeling the wet fabric down my legs, my feet lifting to help, his fingers tickling when they pulled off my sandals. "This is purely in concern for your health," he murmured, opening the dryer and tossing in my jeans, the appliance door hanging open as he returned to me, his eyes traveling from my feet, up the length of my legs, lingering on the white triangle of my panties before he shook his head, a small smile crossing his lips. He stepped closer, his hands shaking a bit as he unbuttoned the front line of my blouse, his hot mouth along the line of my neck as the shirt was carefully removed.

"Nervous?" I teased, my own words shaking slightly as he ran a hand over my newly exposed cleavage.

He smiled, his eyes pulling from my chest to my face. "With you? Always." He wrapped his palms around my waist and lifted, setting me onto the counter, his presence lost for a moment as he added my shirt to the dryer and then - my eyes glued to every movement - stripped himself, the actions quick and fumbled, a laugh coming from my mouth when his feet got tangled in the soggy jeans. By the time he slammed the dryer shut and started it, his glare only made me laugh harder, a hand over my mouth doing nothing to muffle the sound.

"Easy," he growled, stepping forward, grabbing my knees and forcing them apart, the laugh dying in my throat as he leisurely slid his hands up my thighs, his thumbs slowly moving back and forth in their travel. His fingers crawled over my hips, hooking in the edge of my panties, a cheap pair I had picked up in the grocery store, white and plain, his eyes glued to them like they were crotchless lace.

"God, Riley," he breathed. "You are every man's wet dream." He pulled at the edge of the underwear, as if testing their strength, then left them on, his fingers running over the thin fabric, my breath hissing as the pads of his fingers ran down and over my clit, his eyes finding mine when he did the first brush. I leaned back, my hands supporting me on the counter, my legs opening wider, giving myself to him, my confidence growing in his eyes' raw and needy devour of the view. His other hand pulled at the underwear, stretching it tight, the wet press of it against me cold yet stimulating, *everything* stimulating in this moment.

He uttered a curse, his right hand continuing the sweet torture of my clit as his left moved higher, pulling down the top of my bra, another simple white item, anything sexy in the luggage on the forgotten plane. I wondered about the pilot. Did he sit outside these doors, still in the plane, waiting? Is there a chance he'd come in? Push a button and raise the doors, exposing this moment under the bright fluorescence?

My thinking stopped when, with my breasts gently pulled free, hanging out of the top of my bra, Brett's palm scraped over their surface, his hand rougher than normal, a sharp contrast to the gentle play of my clit that was already making me literally pant before him. He ran the back of his nails along my nipples, squeezed the weight of my breasts in his hands, gently tweaked the points as my hips involuntarily twitched, wanting more, his hand responding, a finger sliding under the fabric and moving deeper, into me, the single digit causing a wave of response that had me moaning in his hands.

"You see what you do to me, Riley?" He nodded down, his cock thick and ready, bobbing out and bumping against the counter's edge, just a few inches from me. Shrinkage was a phenomenon that, apparently, didn't affect this man. The knowledge that it was that hard, that ready, without him even touching it, with just him *looking* at me, *touching* me ... I couldn't stop the wave of arousal, the tilt of my need as I reached forward, gripped his shoulder, my scream muffled by my bite into his skin, the thrust of my hips shameless as I ground against his hand, unable to control myself as I came right there on the counter.

His hands didn't stop, carried me through, the moment of his cock's shove into me coming as I fell, my body limp as he held me to him and pounded out every bit of his craving, one of his hands bracing on the counter, his hips a blur, the sound of our slaps and moans and pants echoing through the cavernous space, my body reawakening beneath him, my nails digging into his back, voice begging him for more, a second orgasm so closely behind the first that it felt as if they were tied together with string.

When he came he yelled my name, his hand fisting in my hair, his other hand digging into the cheek of my ass, almost pulling me off the counter in his frenzied need to be as deep and connected as possible. He fully buried himself, his last few fucks short and deep, his voice cracking as he held me to him, his chest heaving, breath ragged against my cheek, his hands holding me in place as if he couldn't bear to let go. "God, Riley." He exhaled. "God, I love you."

chapter 36

It felt strange to be in a big city with Brett, his Porsche SUV taking us through downtown, skyscrapers lining either side, a homeless man staring at me through the window while I glanced nervously away. This was his home, his city, a place so far away from Quincy it might as well have been on a different continent.

I'd never seen him drive before. I watched his hand as it rested on his thigh, the other one hanging off the steering wheel, the glint of his watch red in the reflection of the streetlight. His face in shadow, his movements on the road calm and in control. He was always in control. His need for it was almost OCD, our plans structured around my wishes, the implementation details controlled, to a science, by him. The only break was during sex, when his arousal would blur his control, giving me a wild animal that took with greedy hands and gave with raw passion. I loved those moments, that feeling of power when I had pushed him to the point of breaking, and he turned over all control to me.

"We're about twenty minutes away. Are you hungry? There isn't much to eat in the house."

I shook my head. "I packed a sandwich for the plane." I looked out the window and wondered about his house, if it matched the accommodations we'd always enjoyed on our trips.

Brett's wealth was still a mystery. I remembered Jena's initial research - her estimate of Brett's income. I didn't know how many boats he sold, but couldn't imagine that it was enough for his spending - his exotic vacations every weekend, the plane, the tiny details that lay along every thread of his lifestyle. Brett had never really hidden his money from me; I didn't think he knew how to. It sat in the cut of his suit, in the easy way he settled into a seat and ordered a thousand-dollar bottle of wine. In his casual step into a beachfront mansion in Cabo without even a glance around in appreciation.

A half hour later, he pulled up to a gate, the guard waving him through, the neighborhood one of mini-gates and ivy, the car bumping along cobblestones as we wound through private estates until he came to a stop in front of an iron gate, lions' heads inlaid in the metal.

"Fancy," I remarked.

He glanced over at me. "It's a family house. I didn't earn it. My parents moved to a condo ten years ago, deeded it over." I looked out the window, the house coming into view, and lost a little of my breath.

I didn't care about money. Truly I didn't. But I'd be lying if I said my heart didn't trip a little at the mansion that came into view. It was the house I would have dreamed of if I knew what could exist. A Spanish-style white home with a red tile roof, the enormous size warmed by the planters underneath every window, vibrant flowers spilling from them, putting bursts of color everywhere I looked. Up the walls grew tiny ivy, inset lanterns setting lively shadows over their textured surfaces. "Wow." The word popped out, collecting a chuckle from Brett.

"I've seen it so long I can forget its effect. When you meet Mom, be sure to tell her."

When you meet Mom. I nodded without responding, the car coming to a stop by a large, round fountain, my vantage point now showing a courtyard gate, a view into the house, which seemed to curve around a large pool, all overlooking a dark void which was most likely the ocean.

This house ... it wasn't that of a rich man. This house, this oceanfront estate ... it was WEALTH. Wealth greater than anything in the Smith Bank & Trust coffers. The kind of wealth that kept Rolls Royces in the garage and butlers in the help quarters. I felt suddenly inferior, my flip-flops still wet against the interior of this car, my nails chipped when I reached for the handle.

Brett opened my door, helping me out before popping the trunk and grabbing my bag. "No butler?" I quipped.

He smiled. "Just us. Roughing it this weekend."

I stopped him, pushing against his chest until he hit the car, my bag falling to the ground as he grabbed the offending hand. "Just us?" I repeated, glancing from left to right in the private courtyard. I suddenly wanted to do something, wanted to, in some ways, right the upside-down seesaw I felt on the short end of.

The corner of his mouth turned up, and he released my hand. "Just us."

I reached down, popping the top button of his jeans, and dragged down the zipper. Used the best tool I had and kissed his mouth as I slid my hand inside. Gripped his cock through his underwear as our kiss deepened, his reaction rising against my hand. *Yes.* My confidence soared back to a more comfortable level.

"Riley, wait." His voice was rough yet tender. I paused, letting him pull my hand out of his pants and my body into his chest.

"It's not for the money, is it?" I looked up sharply, at his face, his heart beating a frantic pattern under my hand, his eyes deep in color when they looked down at me. "That's not why you're here. The trips, or the house ... it's not that, right?" I had seen him in a hundred situations, a hundred looks, but never this one, young and vulnerable, like he was twenty instead of thirty-seven. It was shocking to think that, in my moment of insecurity, he was feeling it too, but for the completely opposite reason.

I relaxed in his arms and lifted my hand to his hair. Ran my fingers through it and then over his lips. "The money has nothing to do with this. And, to be honest, I could leave all the travel behind. I'm kind of a homebody, to tell the truth."

A smile hinted, peeked, then stretched over his face. "Really?"

"Really." I smiled. "Now, tell me the truth. Are you just with me for my rocking body?" I pushed off his chest and turned, my arms stretched out, modeling the very sexy jeans and rumpled blouse hanging from my frame.

He laughed, tucking in his cock and zipping up, his eyes taking a slow and obvious leer of my body before he stepped forward, my confident man back, and snagged my bag, slapping my ass and squeezing it. "Absolutely, baby. But I like the things that come outta that sweet little mouth too."

"I think you like putting things in my sweet little mouth too."

He laughed, looped his hand through mine, and we walked into the most beautiful house in the world.

chapter 37

tight (tīt)
(adj.) having close relations; secretive.
"a tight-lipped group"

Brett's friends were odd. A fraternity of hard men, defined by straight posture, strong builds, and matching scowls. I hadn't expected them, his mention of the 'guys' bringing to mind flabby middle-aged men with football jerseys and minivans. I stared at them and had the sudden urge to change, my bathing suit and robe too casual for this group of polo-clad men who surrounded Brett's desk as if they were plotting world domination.

I paused in the doorway of what appeared to be Brett's office. I had followed the sound of male voices, down a long hall, expecting to find a den or media room, the *guys* gathered around a pool table with beers. Instead, they were hunched over Brett's computer, four rigid frames of masculinity, a few affirmative comments thrown out as Brett typed.

My gaze skipped over their faces, and I tried to match the voice I had heard so long ago with one of these faces. Nope. None of these men could have laughed with Brett on a sunny balcony at Atlantis over a cream cheese bagel.

Brett looked up from the center, his hands leaving the keyboard and bracing on the surface, the hunch of his body one that was primal and dominating and *hotaseverlivinghell.* I swallowed as he stared at me, they stared at me, and the study fell silent.

"Can I help you with something?" He didn't smile, didn't straighten, and I stared into his eyes and wondered what the hell I missed. Was this a fantasy football league on crack? A home renovation project they were taking way too seriously?

"No. I'll be out by the pool." I smiled. They scowled. "I'm Riley." I smiled bigger. Waved tentatively. My cheeks were going to fall off at this rate of friendliness.

"Can you give us a moment, Riley?"

"Sure." I stepped back, my wave wilting.

"Please shut the door."

"Okay." I met Brett's eyes, and he smiled. A horrible smile, one that was warm and reassuring and fake. I wrapped my hand around the cold metal knob and pulled, breaking our eye contact, the firm snap of the door in place final and offensive. I stood for a moment, outside, my ear to the wood, but it was too thick, their words impossible to understand.

I walked down the long hall, marble flooring underneath my bare feet, the water bottle in my hand cold, the terrycloth robe floating out a little as I moved. I opened the french doors and stepped out, moving across a sun-lit area and toward the dark pool that stretched before me.

No, that wasn't strange. Five grown men working over a desk, doing secret-secret stuff on a Saturday afternoon. My boyfriend dismissing me as if I were an irritating child interrupting Daddy at work. Not strange at all.

I stretched out on a cushioned chaise, leaving on my cover-up and positioning a pillow under my head. Lying back, I let my mind clearly define the puzzle piece, every bit of that room, that moment. I analyzed and formed the edges and shape of it. Then I worked through my other pieces, tried to make something fit, tried to form a connection with something ... but I failed. The puzzle piece fell, loose and unattached, to the bottom of the pile.

chapter 38
Kitten

"Do I arouse you?" His fingers traveled freely over my skin, soft caresses over my breasts, his hands cupping one of them before traveling over to the second.

"No," I choked out, bucking my back, the bed quiet as I struggled. I can smell my sweat, my arms stretched and cuffed above my head, to the frame. My legs spread slightly, attached to the footboard bars.

"Don't lie, Kitten," he warned. "Lies will only make this last longer. I am a handsome man, no?"

I don't respond, closing my eyes against his face, burying my head to the right, the damp skin cool against my nose.

"I have been told that I am handsome, that I know how to please a woman." I twisted, thrashed as his fingers dragged down my side, my stomach, fingers turning into palms, one of those palms gripping my hip and holding me down.

I begged, my words soft then loud, then screams into the concrete room, a hundred no's uttered as he rubbed soft circles into the wet mat of hair between my legs.

"I will stay here, I will touch you, until you come for me, Kitten. It is inevitable, let it happen. I need to see it."

When it finally happened, every thread in my body failing in fighting it, a cry mixed with tears ripping out, a piece of me inside broke.

chapter 39

I rolled over when the bathroom door opened, flooding the room with light for a brief moment before Brett flipped the switch. Even in the dark, there was illumination from the water, a full moon reflecting over a thousand miles of ocean. Brett's bedroom faced the ocean, a wall of windows giving a million-dollar view of the night waves. He reached out a hand, hit a button on the wall, and a hum sounded, curtains pulling over the view.

"Can you leave them open? I like seeing the waves."

"Sure." He hit another button and the hum stopped. "Just don't blame me when the sunrise wakes you up at five AM." He sat on the edge of the bed and picked up a remote. Pressed a few buttons. I ran a hand over the lines of his back, his skin bare and warm beneath my palm. He carried so much tension there, the muscles underneath my fingers tight and coiled. It was such a beautiful back, so strong and wide. He lay back, interrupting my view and flung out an arm, inviting me in. I curled into his side. "You like it here?"

"It's beautiful." And it was. The city, the neighborhood, his home. Everything the best money could buy. I didn't voice the issues. That it didn't feel like home. That, suddenly, in this zip code, we felt out of sync. I couldn't put my finger on it, just felt, for the first time in our relationship, like I was out of the loop on something. "Who were those guys? In your office? They left before I could meet them."

"Some guys I work with. Friends. I'm sorry... I should have introduced you. I just felt bad about working while you were here."

"It's okay—"

"No. I should have introduced you. I didn't even think … I'm sorry Riley."

"It's not that big of a deal." But it had felt like a big deal to me. Why? What had felt so… suspicious about the whole thing? And, in that moment, my finger found what it had been trying to land on. I felt suspicious.

Of Brett.

The man I'd already given my heart to.

"Why don't we have a cookout tomorrow? I'll invite the guys over, have them bring the girls." Brett was still talking, his voice unnaturally bright.

"The girls?"

"Their girlfriends. You'd love them."

I tried to imagine the girlfriends of those hard men, and the combination we'd make on Brett's pool deck. "It's okay." I ran my hand down his flat stomach, dipping my hand under the silk of his boxer briefs. "I'd rather spend the day with you."

"You sure?" His voice caught when I slid my hand lower, running my fingers over the length of his cock. He tightened his arm around me, pulling me on top of him. "I want to make you happy, Riley."

"You do." I whispered, lowering my mouth to his neck and kissing the scruff there.

He raised his hips and moaned my name as I tightened my hand around his shaft. And, for the next half hour, I lost any thoughts of suspicion.

chapter 40

tight (tīt)
(adj.) well-sealed against intrusion

Somehow, despite my assurances to the contrary, Brett felt the need to invite his friends back over. This time, they brought their girlfriends; all eight individuals apparently had no other plans on a Sunday afternoon. I sat in the shade of an umbrella, nursing a Corona and glanced at the group behind the privacy of my sunglasses.

The men's names were a fog: a Justin, Frank and... I couldn't remember the others. Names had never been my forte. With the women, I made more of an effort. Amy, the brunette by the grill, was dating Justin. She seemed nice, if not a little quiet. Kelly sat next to me, quietly sipping on a margarita, and was married to the man flipping steaks. They had two kids and had been together for four years. I had asked about her children, but she had, with a quiet glance at her husband, stated that they were 'with friends.' Margo and Stacy were in the pool and hadn't said five words to their partners, their main focus on tan development. Now they floated, eyes closed, on recliners in the pool.

"How long have you guys been friends with Brett?" I turned to Kelly with a friendly smile. Her eyes darted from my face to her drink, a shuttered look crossing her face, like I had just asked a deeply personal question.

"A few years," she finally said, her eyes flipping to the outdoor kitchen, where Brett raised his beer to us, a wide smile crossing his face.

I smiled and waved *we're happy over here* and turned back to Kelly, curiosity winning any competition with tact. "Have you met any of Brett's other girlfriends?"

"He hasn't had any," she said quickly, tipping back her glass.

I watched Brett, his eyes skipping between the two of us, his smile dropping slightly. Then he leaned into the man next to him, a telephone-like game occurring, one whisper passing to another, Amy receiving the secret message and heading toward us, her strides quick and confident, her smile breezy when she flopped down in the chair across from me. "What'd I miss?" she asked. "Anything exciting?"

Kelly looked away, and I leaned forward. "I was just asking about Brett's exes. How much I had to compete with." I grinned as if I didn't care about the answer, as if I wasn't pumping strangers for intel like a crazy, insecure woman.

Her smile fell, then rose again, as if it was programmed to reset. "Well, that's easy," she recovered. "He hasn't had any. At least not as long as I've known him. What do you do in Quincy, Riley?"

I ignored the question, intent on knowing *something* more. "Why'd the guys come over yesterday? It looked like they were working on something."

Dead silence. Suddenly, Breezy Amy had nothing to say. I looked from one to the other, Kelly's neck twisting even further away, Amy's jaw working open and closed with no words coming out. I felt like I had just stepped on a landmine and had no idea why. Finally, Amy's voice box worked. "The guys are always getting together."

"Guy stuff," Kelly said dully.

"Yeah!" Amy said brightly. "Guy stuff. I stay out of it."

"Me too." Kelly looked up, a false smile pasted in my direction. "Sports stuff bores me."

"Are your guys also in sales?" God, I can't believe I forgot their names.

Another uncomfortable pause.

"Sort of," Amy finally managed while Kelly just held her smile.

I out-faked her in the smile department, then tipped back my Corona, my seed of suspicion growing roots.

CHAPTER 41
BRETT

tight (tīt)
(adj.) disciplined or professional, well coordinated
"a tight ship"

After we gave Marcia a clean bed and nursed her back to life, after I watched her trembling hand hold my phone and call her parents, I became a man obsessed. With saving these women, with diving into the guts of this beast and ripping every entrail out. I thought it would be easy, thought that I could hire a few Navy SEALS and clean up the issue in the course of weeks. Envisioned, with the few rays of optimism that remained in my heart, that we'd find or avenge Elyse. I rolled up my cufflinks and waded in next to the men. Became, my large fortune in hand, one of the largest purchasers of women in the business. I became notorious, whispers of my cruelty and insatiable need for more flowed through the underground, fed by carefully planted stories and rumors. Plus, there were my buying habits. I bought anything - every age, race, and size. Our first year we bought 62 women. The second, 104. The third, 129. I opened a house in Miami for rehabilitation and staffed it with a medical team, psychologists, and six caregivers. I saved as many as I could, my weekends spent in the air, the Caribbean and Central America my feeding ground, the thousand miles surrounding where Elyse disappeared canvassed as thoroughly as possible.

Every saved soul was a pebble into the stream that was my broken heart. I threw every pebble in and hoped the water would dam, hoped the hurt would fade, hoped the memories would fade. But the stream never dried, the hurt never ceased, and my pain never healed.

Until I met Riley. I watched her blush and take the slippers. Felt the brush of her hand as we walked. Heard the gasp of her inhale as I thrust. Became lost in her face when she orgasmed around my cock, felt the warmth of her smile when we shared a joke. Felt alive from her enthusiasm for life and living. Enjoyed peace as I watched the sigh of her chest as she slept. I met Riley and - for the first time since Elyse's disappearance—felt the first hint of something more, of a life outside of my rabid search for a woman who was already dead.

chapter 42
Kitten

"Why do you ask me so many questions?"

"I'm gathering information." He uncrossed and recrossed his legs, this time at the ankle, sitting back in his chair and folding his arms on his chest.

I sat on my bed, the handcuffs and bindings removed some time ago. I had, in ways, lost my fight. Could be trusted to sit without attacking, to sleep without destroying my room or myself. There was only so much trouble I could get into in the room, the reason for the cuffs more about domination than anything. Thinking about and remembering the long hours, I rubbed my wrists.

"Let's play a game, Kitten."

"I don't like your games."

"Well, this one is different. It has a prize." He grinned widely, like he had just granted me my freedom.

He wanted me to ask. I could feel the words *what prize* shoving my tongue down, lips apart but I stayed mute. Sat on my bed and examined my toenails. Punished him in the way that hurt him the most, silence - a withholding of reaction, of information, of content to write down in his fucking notebook. I clamped my lips shut and picked at a spot on my big toe.

Seconds turned into a minute. I examined, he sat, seconds ticked. Finally he sighed, a big loud guttural sound that stretched out unnecessarily. I waited, not looking, not responding, my peripheral vision showing movement of some kind. Finally, I broke, turning to him, my eyes falling on a brightly colored gift.

"You want this, Kitten?" he asked, lifting up the box and shaking it.

"Is it a cell phone?" I asked, releasing my toe.

"No."

"Then no. Unless it's a cell phone, or a 'Get Out of Jail Free' card, I'm not interested."

"Make me happy, Kitten, and you can have this. It will be the only pretty thing in this room, the only thing that is *yours*."

"You call me Kitten so that I form an emotional connection to you, isn't that what you said?"

"Yes."

"You should probably know that every time you say that word I want to either punch you in the face or vomit."

That sentence earned me a line in his notebook, his pen scratching across the surface, the present wobbling a little on his knee. It was a hot pink rectangular box, the kind that men's dress shirts come in. It's probably clothes. What an idiot. I'd probably answer every question in his notebook for a TV with Netflix.

"This could be a good step for us, Kitten. Movement forward. Let's play, okay?"

"No."

"So, you won't help me to earn this gift?"

"No."

"Have you ever studied dog training, Kitten?"

I didn't answer.

"There is a body of opinion that training a dog should be all positive reinforcement, manipulation with praise and treats. I had a theory I wanted to put into practice and have done so with you, Kitten."

I stopped fidgeting.

"You've successfully completed phase one with me, and given me a lot of information, Kitten. For that, I will *give* you this present. One last gift from me. But from now on, you will not eat well, or receive anything, unless you *earn* it. And anytime you disobey me, you will be punished. If you speak back, you will be punished. If you do not answer my questions, or please me, you will be punished. He stood, the soles of his shoes scraping the concrete as he walked over to me. I watched the package as he set it down softly on the bed before me. "Enjoy this, Kitten. Thank you for proving my hypothesis that positive reinforcement is not enough. Sleep well. Tomorrow is a big new day."

I stared at the wrapped gift as he walked out the door.

That night, I couldn't sleep. I stared at it, recounted every request of his that I had turned down. Every question I had refused. Every statement that I had given a sarcastic response to. A hundred mini-tests. All that I had failed.

Hours later, emotionally exhausted, I tried to squeeze the gift through my bars. When it didn't fit, I squashed it, punching on it until it popped through the bars and landed, unopened, on the other side, skittering to a stop next to a bag of mulch.

It was Phase One's final act of rebellion.

chapter 43

3 weeks before

I gripped the handles of my bag—a new one—purchased a month earlier in Cabo. Hefted it over my shoulder and stepped toward the plane, Abe nodding at me, the sun making his silver hair glint. "Good morning, ma'am."

"Good morning. Smooth weather?"

"Yep. Clear skies."

I smiled tightly, passing him my bag and jogging up the steps, a paperback in hand. I'd flown with Abe fifteen times now. He certainly seemed competent, touching down in last week's storm without disaster. But I still got nervous, stepping into the death trap, even if it did come complete with elegant trappings and a minibar.

I texted Brett, let him know we were departing, and buckled in. Reclined my seat and tried to relax. In two hours, we would touch down in Lauderdale, where we'd pick up Brett, and fly another half hour to Jamaica. The next three days would be spent on the beach before returning home—Brett to his, me to mine. A long distance apart. Each separation was starting to get harder. I stayed on the plane when it landed at FLL, moving aside the curtain and watching as Brett jogged across the pavement, a leather bag in hand, a polo stretched across his strong shoulders, jeans hugging thighs that I'd soon be astride. He opened the door himself, the change in cabin pressure bringing a gust of fresh air and, minutes later, the tousled head of the man who I was in love with.

"Hey babe." He leaned over my seat, placing both hands on the armrest, and gave me a deep kiss. "I missed you."

I grinned. "It's been four days." Only four days since we were on the beach in Cancun. My skin was hitting a level of tan it'd never known in October. Note to single women everywhere: date a man who works in exotic locales. I didn't know how I'd ever go back to the unexciting men of Quincy.

"Four days felt like forever. How much trouble is this weekend getting you into at work?"

I shrugged. "I'll sort it out." I'd have to. I'd left that afternoon to a glare from Anita, my manager. Being the town's only FA could only get me so much leeway, and I had spoiled them by not taking a vacation day in two years. The initial support over my new relationship had quickly soured into polite disapproval over the last months.

I glanced out the window, my hands tightening on the armrest as the plane accelerated down the runway.

***

Before Brett, I would have called Jamaica paradise. Emerald blue water, white sand, palm-treed islands everywhere you turned. Stick a frozen margarita in front of me and I would have been in bliss.

But now, with Brett-quality travel underneath my sarong's belt, my eyes saw things differently. They picked up on the gaunt barefoot youth that scowled at our car. They noted the armed guards who stood before the Ritz Carlton's gates, their machine guns and bulletproof vests sending a shiver of alarm through me.

"Is this a bad area?" My eyes met one of the guards', and he nodded curtly, no smile given. Our car continued on, a directional arrow for our hotel ahead. I wondered briefly why we weren't staying at the Ritz. It seemed ridiculous to fly private and then skimp on hotel accommodations, especially for Brett, a man who spent freely.

He shrugged. "It's Jamaica." Like that answered it.

"Why'd we come here?"

"Business." He leaned over, nuzzling a spot above my collarbone before moving to my lips and taking a long kiss.

"Is that why we're staying at Luchen?"

He pulled back, studied my eyes, his mouth curving. "You're stuck on the Ritz, right? You'd rather stay there?"

I laughed, trying to play off my comment. "No, I don't care where we stay. I was just asking."

"The men I'm meeting want girls. Luchen is where the college girls come to party. They are simple men, more interested in bikinis than thread count. I'm just following their wishes."

I frowned. "Great. Something for me to think about every time you are off on 'business.'"

His hand stole down, in between my thighs. "I don't want those girls, Riley. *This* is the only thing I have on my mind." He drew his hand up, cupping my panties, his fingers teasing me through the cloth. I exhaled, trying to maintain composure.

"You sure?"

"I'm sure." He looked toward the driver. "How far away are we?"

"Five minutes, Mr. Jacobs. Maybe less."

"Five minutes." His eyes returned to mine as he threatened me with the time, a digit starting a steady roll back and forth over my clit. I closed my eyes, my back involuntarily curving against the seat, making me more available to his hand. "Five minutes and then I'll fuck you so well you'll never doubt that again."

chapter 44

Our second day in Jamaica, and I was alone in the hotel bed. I stared at the clock. 11:48 PM. We had gone to dinner. Then had drinks in the bar. Then Brett excused himself, heading downstairs to meet with clients.

I was noticing a pattern.

Every trip—one or two nights, Brett had business. Not the entire night, just for a few hours, at the time in which nothing good happened. I wasn't used to this, the men of my town, of my upbringing, were the Southern gentlemen type. We didn't have late night parties, didn't return home at two AM. My town was too small for secrets or affairs. You farted in your living room, and folks in Ken's Deli were talking about it the next morning. So I was out of my element with Brett's activities.

I understood that not all business dealings were the handshake-over-cow-fence transactions that I grew up with. I understood that Brett's clients were flashy men who chased women and fished with equal vigor, thinking nothing of downing tequila before writing a five million dollar check. That didn't mean this smelled right. Didn't mean that—just one time—he couldn't bring me along. I sat up, swung my feet off the bed and thought.

I could just call him out on it. I'd come close multiple times. Made enough offhand remarks to understand that he wasn't interested in discussing it. In our relationship, this was the only hitch. The only thing that gave me pause. Was it worth chasing down?

I walked to the bathroom and looked into the mirror. Ran my fingers over my lips, the surface still tender from the rough passion that Brett exhibited. I was a pretty girl; I knew that. A little heavy, but Momma called it 'curvy,' so it worked. Brett had never made me feel anything but gorgeous. Never gave me any reason to doubt his loyalty or attraction. Yet there were these nights. History had taught me that he wouldn't return for hours, his location unknown. I wondered if he had taken out a hotel car, or if he stayed on location. Given the apparent violence in Jamaica, I guessed he was still at the resort, especially since his clients were staying here. I opened the closet door and ran my hands across the hangers. All dresses I'd worn for him before. My glamorous outfit selection was pretty thin, my budget not big enough to expand it. Brett had tried to take me shopping, but I'd held him off. Maybe later. For now, these four dresses did the job. I tapped a finger along the fabric.

I should go back to bed. Stare at the ceiling and let my mind explore all sorts of possibilities. Blink some. Maybe reward myself with some bottled water if I got through an hour without pulling any hair out.

Instead I tugged at the closest hanger, withdrawing the red mini-dress. I stared at it for a moment, then hung it on the towel rod and pulled off my T-shirt.

***

God, I was too old for this shit. I waved a hand before my face in an attempt to break through the smoke, a futile move, the smog parting only to re-attack. I coughed, stepping farther inside, and looked around. Tops of heads, that was all that I saw, crammed into this club like sardines. Behind me, a body brushed by, a male hand taking a liberal journey of my ass. I tried to spin, tried to glare, but the press of bodies fought against me, moving me deeper into the throng. Twentysomethings everywhere, all showing tan skin and carrying drinks, one bump sloshing half a beer across my wrist. I shook my hand and tried to look for an out. Didn't they have fire codes in this country? Heaven forbid an emergency occurred. I felt a bit of claustrophobia at the thought, and took a few shallow breaths, counting to five and forcing myself forward. *I can't go back. Maybe I can go through.*

It didn't make sense. Why, in the name of boat sales everywhere, would he meet with clients *here*? But I'd just walked through the other areas of the hotel, everything closed with the exception of this club. He *had* to be here, in this place where no conversation could be had, a place where sexuality and alcohol seemed to be the only game in town.

Forget finding Brett. I couldn't take another minute of this; it wasn't worth it. I just wanted to be back in the quiet of our room, with a working remote and fresh air. I could do secret reconnaissance at another resort, at another time. Preferably in a place where the locals didn't stare me down like my breasts were made of gold, equal parts hatred and interest in their eyes. I stopped being polite and started to push through the crowd, aiming for the closest wall, not hearing my name until it was screamed at close range.

I tried to look, but could only crane my neck so far, my attempt ending when a strong hand wrapped around my wrist and yanked me right, through a dancing couple, and into the hard chest of Brett. His other arm wrapped around my back, holding me in place, tight to his body, the crowd closing in. I looked up into his face, his eyes glaring down at me as if I had done something wrong. He lowered his head to my ear, his words barely discernable. "What are you doing here?"

"I was looking for you!" I shouted the words, the music's beat stealing them away. He pulled back enough to see my eyes, then lowered his mouth back to my ear.

"You shouldn't be here."

"Why?" This time I matched his glare. Fine. *This* was where this would happen.

"It's dangerous. Go back to the room."

I laughed. It may have been a mistake. His eyes flashed in a way I'd never seen. A new level of anger. A shriek of surprise came out when he picked me up, underneath my knees and arms, curling me against his chest and shouldering us through the crowd, my kicking heels bumping strangers, my left hand hooking around his neck to protect my head while I pounded on his chest with my other hand. "Let me down!" I yelled in his ear, his face unresponsive, dark stubbornness on it as he plowed through the crowd.

Our combined bulk broke through the bodies and backed through a door set into the wall, the music muffled in the dark hall where we ended up. I was finally free, my legs released without warning, right before he pinned me against the wall, his other hand braced next to my head. He waited for the door to swing shut, the hall quieting to a level where shouting was not necessary.

"Now," he spoke slowly and tightly, "tell me what the *fuck* you planned to accomplish by coming here tonight."

I bristled, trying to straighten off the wall, his hand pressing against my chest and easily keeping me in place. "I didn't think I needed a reason to come see my *boyfriend*."

"You think this is a game?" he thundered. "Girls disappear from this resort all the time. Just now, I carried you through that crowd, you were screaming bloody murder, and not *one* person gave it a second look. What if it hadn't been me? What if it had been someone else? Someone who carried you into this hall and raped you? Killed you?" His gaze moved down, my face flushing at the realization that my dress, due to his carry, had ridden up to almost my waist.

"Jesus Christ, Riley," he groaned, his voice softening, his hand leaving the wall to run up my thigh. "I can see your fucking panties." He slipped his hand underneath the dress, caressing the skin of my hip before moving to the front, my hand grabbing his wrist before it moved lower. If he touched me, I was done. I knew it; it'd happened too many times before. He'd learned every button I had and just how to push them. If he wanted to, he could fuck me right here in this hall, and I wouldn't be able to say a word to stop it. Despite being mad at him. Despite not wanting to want it.

"Stop." I pressed on his wrist, resisted its movement.

His head came up, his eyes meeting mine. "Tell me you don't want it."

"I don't want it."

He stepped closer, sliding his fingers under the top of my panties, my fight against the movement futile, my strength no match for his, his eyes tight on mine as his fingers slid over the thin patch of hair and pressed inside of me. I closed my eyes, sank a little against the wall, my legs spreading slightly on their own accord.

"Liar," he whispered. "Open your eyes, beautiful. Open your eyes and tell me why you are here."

"I told you."

"Yeah, you also told me you don't want this."

I opened my eyes, glared at him, the action muted by a push of his finger, my eyes dropping closed as I weakly tried to push against his hand, not even sure why I was bothering.

"You're here because you don't trust me." He unzipped his pants, my eyes widening at the action.

"What are you doing?"

"I'm about to fuck you."

"No." I shoved against him. "I'm going upstairs, and I'm packing. You can fuck one of these sluts."

His hand was hard when it palmed my cheek, holding me back, his legs straddling my feet and caging me into place. "Listen to me, Riley." My struggle did nothing to stop the bare brush of his cock against my thighs. I clenched my legs for protection and avoided his eyes. "You think I'm here for *them*?" He tilted his head to the club. "I haven't stopped thinking about you since I left the room. You've been the only thing on my mind since I saw you five months ago in that casino. I'm steps away from putting a ring on that perfect little finger just to convince you to move to me. I am not here to *fuck* anyone except you."

I stared straight ahead and struggled to keep my face passive. "Let me go."

"You don't mean that," he whispered, pressing closer to me, his mouth dropping to my neck, softly pressing kisses into the skin there. I blinked, tears hot on the edges of my eyes, stinging bits of weakness. I didn't even know why I was crying. I didn't have a good reason, didn't even know what emotion to feel right now, just that I was one raw ball of nerves. I hugged him to me, wanting to hide the tears, the action pressing his pelvis tighter, his exposed cock pushing into the tight opening between my thighs. He hissed against my neck, gently grabbing the skin with his teeth as he rocked his hips once, sliding it out and then in. I clenched my thighs tighter and reached down, wrapping my hand around the length of him. I squeezed, his head coming off my neck, his hand brushing the hair away from my face, his mouth greedy as it found mine. I grabbed it a little tighter as he thrust against my grip, his breath puffing out in between our kisses.

There was something so untouchably hot about having him in my hand, in that hallway, the vibration of the club at my back, the chance of interruption, the forbidden kiss of a man who, apparently, didn't give a damn.

We were quiet, no words to say, just the rustle of our clothes, the hard blows of his breath, the sounds of his breakage. He pulled his mouth off mine and leaned his forehead against the wall. "You won't fuck me?" he panted.

"No," I whispered, squeezing tighter, his hips continuing their thrust into my grip, the speed increasing, his breath growing ragged at my response.

"Then I'm about to fucking come everywhere."

I debated stepping aside, letting him blow his load all over the club's floor, considered parting my legs and letting him, for a few deep thrusts, push inside. Instead, I squatted, keeping my hand on his shaft, and covered his head with my mouth.

The sounds, as they ripped from his throat, the shake of his thigh underneath my hand...

It was beautiful and uncontrolled and all for me.

chapter 45

Brett didn't do any more business after that. He rubbed sunscreen on my back, had roses delivered to the room, and woke me up with kisses. We didn't discuss the club or our mini-fight. Looking back, I should have brought it up, should have pushed on that soft spot until my finger broke through to the truth. I could have, and our relationship would have survived, would have strengthened. But I didn't. I rolled over in his bed, took his kisses and roses and *I love yous* and ignored it. I was too afraid of what I didn't know. Too afraid that, if I thought about it hard enough, I'd find something wrong and I didn't want to damage the first true love I had ever had. He had mentioned *proposing*. I didn't know if he meant it, but I knew how I felt at the words. A hundred *whatifs* bounding through my mind and collecting bits of excitement and love along the way. This had become *something*—not a relationship to kick to the curb over paranoid suspicions. I needed to analyze it once I was back home. Make sure I was prepared for when the moment came, *if* the moment came. It'd only been five months; we weren't naïve kids. I was thirty-two. He a thirty-seven year old man who'd never been married. I wasn't expecting him to drop down on one knee after a few romantic escapades. But still.

My stick-my-head-in-the-sand bliss lasted until 4 AM, when I got up to pee, Brett's body not stirring as I gently rolled out of bed and walked to the bathroom. The wood floors in the room squeaked, like tattletale elves, the noises unnoticeable during the day, thundering at night. I flushed, then washed my hands, a nightlight putting an upward glow on my face. A horrible angle, it highlighted every wrinkle, every bag. I looked fifty, my stringy hair hanging around my face like old curtains around a dirty window. Thirty-two. Still young, but God, I didn't look it. Not right now, not right here. I looked down, at my hands, red from the hot water, my fingers gripping the edge of the sink. Why was he in that club? How many nights had I sat alone in hotel rooms thinking he was working? And what had he been doing instead? My eyes moved from my hands to the counter. To the white towel laid out, Brett's items set neatly next to mine. I picked up his toothbrush, a silver electric one. It was heavy. Felt expensive, like every other thing in Brett's life. I set it down. Moved to the electric razor. This was older, worn. I had joked with him about the razor, told him I finally knew what to buy him for Christmas. He'd shook his head. "That was my father's. Invest in lingerie instead." He'd smiled, kissed my cheek, and I'd understood. Now, I hefted it in my hand. Thought. Considered. At what point am I a patsy, and at what point am I paranoid? I set down the razor and leaned forward. Stared into my eyes. Closed them. Opened them. I sighed, settling back on my heels and reaching for my makeup bag. Pulled out a Ziploc bag and pulled out my Q-tips. Popped off the top of the razor and dumped the clippings into the bag. Zipped it shut and replaced the razor's top. Set it down.

For a short time, I considered becoming a cop. It was over a decade ago, when I was still dating John, and we had this romantic notion that we would both go into law enforcement and work alongside my father, solving Quincy's crimes and stealing kisses in between high-profile cases. I read some forensics books. Tagged along with Dad for a few weeks. Did some ride-alongs. Quickly realized that being a cop in Quincy was comparable to babysitting drunken toddlers. Changed my career path to psychology. Then ten more times before I settled on finance. It was over a decade ago, but I remembered reading about a murder investigation that was solved with DNA pulled from razor clippings. I hesitated, then grabbed the mini toothpaste tube with a Kleenex.

Collecting prints and DNA. Had my suspicions really come to this?

I'd give my father permission to run them both through the system. He'd be clean. I knew it. My polished, beautiful man wasn't doing anything wrong, at least not that my father would find. I was certain of it. This would just close one door and give me a little more information. This would just give me a little peace of mind.

I knew what I felt. I loved him. But I didn't know him. And I didn't trust him. The man I had fallen for hid something. I could feel it, slipping into bed with us at night, slithering up my bare legs, looking for a vulnerable place to bite.

I wanted, needed, to know that secret.

I crawled quietly back into bed, the soft sighs of Brett comforting. And the next night, I packed my bag and we headed back. I landed back home a little after nine, the plane empty, Brett dropped in Lauderdale where we fueled up.

"Thanks, Abe." I ducked through the door and down the steps, waving through the glass at the airport's desk clerk, her acknowledgement barely visible through the dusty glass. Behind me, I heard the hum of propellers as the plane rolled on. It felt good to be home, it felt as if I'd been gone a month and needed to play catch-up with my thoughts.

I hefted my bag open and dug for my keys. *Found 'em.* I popped the trunk and tossed in the bag. The bag containing Brett's DNA. Funny how that made the tote that much heavier. Glanced quickly around to make sure no abductors were lurking in the shadows, then unlocked and got into the car. Stifled a grin when I thought of Brett's concern about my house. Abductors in Quincy. Another thing that wouldn't ever happen. Our worst crime last year was when Beau Thomas exposed himself to old Mrs. Huddleston in the library. She snapped a picture and posted it on the bulletin board with a small rose sticker over his private parts, 'Tiny' written in her delicate script beside the photo. The police came, scratched their heads over the situation, and finally decided the photo was punishment enough, provided Mrs. Huddleston would leave it up for a year. Mrs. Huddleston did one better, getting it published in the Quincy Quarterly as well. Now, every soul in Quincy knew how perverted, and underendowed, Beau Thomas was. I already knew; I'd found out in sixth grade.

Yeah, Quincy wasn't Jamaica; we didn't have armed guards and disappearing spring breakers, but it didn't mean I was stupid. I was fine in that club despite Brett's posturing. I was fine in this town without his directives. I put the car into drive and pulled out of the empty lot.

chapter 46
Kitten

I knew, when I was taken, that my parents would look for me. Brett would look for me. I held on to that with every fiber of my soul. But that fiber, along with my sanity, unwrapped a little bit each day, a wisp of thread at a time, the slow uncurling of the person I used to be. I fought it, clung with greedy hands and stubborn retorts, to my old self, to the memories that I had. But with each new day, each new experience, I lost a bit of them. And he didn't help. He stood over me with his fucking clipboard and pushed for *moremoremore* of my soul, was never satisfied, would never be satisfied, not until I was fully worshipping at his feet, my body and soul offered up without hesitation. I struggled, I fought, I clung to the memory of Brett. He loved me. He would find me.

"Come here." The voice came from across my cell, from the chair where my tormentor sat, his legs slightly spread, naked thighs leading the way to his cock. It stood before me, upright and beckoning, the shaft bobbing at me as if to wave.

I looked away, my hands fisting on the sheets. He had once mentioned dog training, had taken that psychology to heart. I felt like Bill Murray in *Groundhog Day*, this event a complete repeat of the last six or seven encounters. He asked, I refused, he beat me. Today, my body sore and broken, I stood. Walked with tender steps to him. Stopped before him, my eyes down.

Phase Two had stretched countless days, months. Maybe even years. I had, through the pain and deprivation, further lost track of time. I also had broken on a few things. I now called him Master.

Assumed subservient positions. Kept my head and eyes down. I actually liked that part of it. Not having to look at him. Not until the moment that he grabbed my jaw and forced my eyes to his.

I woke from Brett's touch, his hand soft on my jaw, brushing over it so lightly, a whisper of contact as I curled into his hand. "Hey beautiful," he whispered, his eyes on mine, his leg wrapping around mine and pulling me closer.

I blinked, the dark room hiding much of his features, my groggy mind trying to place our location. My house. I recognized the padded headboard, the dark grey comforter that hung off my bare shoulder. "What time is it?" My voice cracked, groggy from sleep.

"Around three."

I snuggled closer and let my eyes close, resting my head on his chest. "And why are you waking me up?"

"I didn't mean to wake you. I just couldn't keep myself from touching you." I felt the soft press of his lips against my hair, the brush of his fingers across my hip, the hook of his foot beneath my leg. We were completely fused, his body a warm glove, his chest gently rising and falling underneath my head.

"I love you," he whispered.

"I love you too."

I pulled from the past when I felt his fingers, the lean of his body forward as he pulled my face up. I yielded under the pressure, lifting my chin and looking up into his eyes. He slid his hand from my chin to my throat, his thumb gently running along the tender muscles before he continued further back, cupping the back of my neck and pulling me forward. "Keep your eyes open," he ordered, his hand hard. "Look at me when you suck my cock."

I obeyed, held the contact as I slid down the shaft.

I held the contact as he lifted his hips, thrusting into my mouth, my eyes watering at the depth.

I held the contact as he called me a good cocksucker and asked if I liked his taste.

I held the contact as I clamped my jaw down on his most sensitive organ as hard as I could.

chapter 47

2 weeks before

The coffee at Sunshine sucked. But it had for sixteen years, and everyone quit bitching about it a decade ago. I pushed the white mug away from me and mentally vowed not to touch it until the food arrived.

"When will you see him again?" my father's voice creaked from a lifetime of smoking.

"Two weeks. He's got something this weekend and I'm going to work on Saturday. Try to get back in Anita's good graces. Speaking of which, I've got to leave here by eight."

He shrugged, taking a sip from his cup. "What made you give me that?"

I looked into his eyes. "Just a feeling. Something is off. I'm just trying to figure it out. I figured extra information couldn't hurt."

He sighed, reaching for the creamer and adding a little to his cup. "I shouldn't be drinking this," he remarked. "Dr. Bonner told me to cut back on my caffeine. My blood pressure's high again."

I held the gaze and our table fell quiet in the minute before a young redhead approached our table, order pad in hand. We put in our breakfast order, then she left.

Finally, he spoke. "So, tell me about this man. What you do know. Then I'll share my goods." My dad leaned forward, his fingers rubbing his knuckles, the extra weight on his frame pushing the table slightly in my direction. An imposing man, despite the years and the stress, his full head of silver hair stuck in the buzz cut he'd worn my entire life.

"Brett Jacobs. He's a boat—yacht—salesman, but seems to make a lot of money. As you know, he travels a lot. He's single, never been married, no kids."

"Do you want kids?" Brett asked, his hand sliding under the sheet and curving around my hip. I opened my eyes, blinking the impending sleep away.

"I'd love kids." I reached out, putting a hand on his chest. "What about you?"

"Kids are good. Preferably sooner. Before I get too old." He smiled, the scant light catching on the shadows of his face.

"You know the problem with kids." I sighed, frowning.

"What?"

"The process to make them." I roll onto my stomach, away from him, his hand dropping from my hip, the bed shifting as I felt him move closer.

"What's the issue with that?" His words, close to my ear, his breath hot on my neck. I smiled against the pillow.

"It's so... boring," I mumbled.

Then I felt him, bare and hard, his body atop me, his hands like hot stones on my skin, and I shrieked into the dark room and there was nothing boring about it.

"What else?"

I shrugged. "That's about it. I won't bore you with his eating habits or taste in movies."

"I know I'm protective of you."

I stopped playing with the creamers and looked up at him. "What's wrong?" That sentence...from my father. My stomach twisted in a way I hadn't felt since I was young.

"You care for him, I know that. But you must have known something was up or else you wouldn't have let me run full course with this."

"You've done background checks on every man I've ever dated." And he had. It had been embarrassing. Invasive. Annoying. Never appreciated. Not until Brett. Brett was the first time I had willingly turned over a partner's DNA. Willingly met with my father and *wanted* to know what he had found.

"He's lying." The words flat and without enjoyment.

I swallowed. Pulled my hands off the table and hid them on my lap. Pushed at my cuticles, a habit I had squashed a few years earlier. "About what?"

"Hell, just 'bout everything."

***

Lying about everything.

Bullshit.

Impossible.

I knew this man. Loved this man. Kissed and fucked and wanted him, not just physically but emotionally. I wanted to go to bed with his arms around me every night. I wanted to walk down an aisle and look in his eyes. I wanted him to hold my hand as we watched a pregnancy stick. I wanted to watch wrinkles multiply and years pass and build a lifetime of memories with him.

He was not lying about everything. He loved me. I closed my mouth and watched my father begin to speak.

"His real name is Brett Betschart. He doesn't sell yachts; he manufactures them. Or, more specifically, he owns the company that manufactures them. He seems like he makes more money because he does make more money. Millions more. Hell, the type of money I don't even understand." He reaches for his front pocket and pulls out a can of dip.

Millions more. The plane, the house, the ... everything. It made sense, so much sense, and I felt a burst of relief. *That's* what was wrong. That was all! Thank God. Only... "Why would he lie about that?"

He shrugged. "Men lie about a lot of things. God made us imperfect creatures. "

I leaned back, my mind working over the weekend we met. It was a stupid, *pointless* lie. Why lie about your name? Why lie about your job? Except... if he wasn't in sales, if he owned the company ... there's no need for the late meetings, for wining and dining the buyers. There's really no need for *any* trips at all.

"Does he have a record?"

"No. But all I ran was his prints. The DNA'll take a few weeks; it'll show if he's ever been connected with a crime. But the chances of that are slim."

He's holding something back. I wet my lips. "What else?"

"That's about it, pumpkin."

"*About*? What aren't you saying?" I leaned forward, snagged the empty dip can from his fingers, and stared into his eyes.

"Just be careful with him, Riley." He met my eyes, dark brown clouds of worry.

"Screw that. You aren't going cryptic on me. What aren't you saying?"

"Let me get some callbacks. Find out more before I go shooting my big mouth off." He sat back, looking right and smiling at the waitress, eyeing the plates she set down. "Thank you, Jeannie."

I ignored the platter of pancakes, my nails digging into the Skoal can. "Dad." My father, the one who's run off every man in town, and here he was, being coy and mysterious about the man who owned my heart.

"Eat your breakfast. I told you what I know. If I find out more, I'll tell you then."

"Tell me *now*. I don't care if it's accurate. Just tell me."

He stabbed a piece of sausage and lifted it to his mouth. Chewed for a long minute. "He's been questioned a few times. In disappearances of girls - the type who run drugs. Nothing's stuck, but his name's in more files than I feel comfortable with. That's why I'm thinking the DNA will be a bust. There's been no arrests, just questioning. That's all I got. I've got calls into a detective in Fort Lauderdale to find out more."

My pancakes suddenly lost all appeal. I'd been expecting a secret family, a wife in the Hamptons, a love child. This was unexpectedly worse. "What happened to the girls?"

"The two I found out about? Chances are they're running from warrants, are being hidden by a drug cartel somewhere. No bodies have shown up."

Drug Cartel. Bodies. The ugliest response in the world.

chapter 48

"Is everything okay?" Brett's voice was lowered, almost a hush, and I wondered who was around him. Less than twenty-four hours after breakfast with my father, and he could tell. That was a good sign for our relationship. A bad sign for any future I had as an actress.

Is everything okay? I once asked my last boyfriend that. I thought those three words were the death sentence to a relationship. Was that what this was? A death sentence? I needed a few days, a hundred hours of silence, my butt in a rocker, on my front porch, to think. Muse through this all and come out the other side.

"It's fine." I smiled, forgetting he couldn't see me. "I'm just a little under the weather."

"We should talk about Jamaica. What happened."

Yes, we should. But I didn't want to. Not about Jamaica. I couldn't take any extra conversation, my mouth already fighting against the words screaming inside my head. *Why did you lie? Why hide your identity?* I needed to hang up the phone before I said something I regretted and looked certifiable. I swallowed. "I've got to run, Brett. My next appointment is here."

I should have known he wouldn't let it go that easy. I shouldn't have been surprised when, six hours later, he landed in Quincy.

***

I was on a walk with Miller, my hands fisted in the Browning jacket, puffs of dirt following each step of my sneakers, when I saw the cloud of dust. No one snuck up on anyone on a dirt road. Not in the daytime. Any car left a dust trail a quarter-mile long. I stopped and watched the car. Miller continued on, his head down as he sniffed at an offending wildflower. It was an old sedan, a tan four-door, its frame shaking across the ruts in my road, and it slowed down way before my mailbox, the turn signal blinking brightly through the approaching dusk.

And I knew. Didn't even wonder, didn't guess. I *knew* it was him. And, for one long moment, my feet rooted in the dirt, I didn't want him there. I wasn't ready to pretend, certainly wasn't ready to confront, didn't want anything other than to trudge up my steps, draw a hot bath, and drown my sorrows in a glass of wine.

Could I do it? Could I walk in my house and hide my nerves? Could I wrap my arms around his neck and laugh off his concerns? Could I swallow my feelings and play the part of normal?

I didn't want to confront him. Not now, when all I had was some hearsay from my father. All based on illegally obtained DNA. Well, maybe it wasn't *illegally* obtained but my methods certainly had been on the north side of crazy. He'd probably be mad, offended. I'd counter back that he'd been lying. We'd fight. He'd storm out. And I'd have no more of an idea what was going on than before.

Thank God for long driveways. For dusk, which allowed me to hide in the shadows and watch him try my door. He pulled out a phone and called my cell. It wasn't on me; it was back in the house and I saw the moment he began to panic. To worry, his fist pounding on the door. *He loves me.* He had to. He said it, and I could see it. He wouldn't worry like this if he didn't. His frame wouldn't be so stiff, his movements so quick, his hand so rough as it gripped at his hair. *I love him.* I had to. I knew I did. Otherwise my steps wouldn't be quickening, I wouldn't be calling. I wouldn't be running to the man instead of hauling tail in the opposite direction.

When he saw me, his shoulders dropped, his face relaxed, his arms reached out and wrapped around me. He buried his head in my neck and squeezed me tight, the bump of Miller's body comical as he wound his way through our legs. "I was worried," he said.

"You're here."

"Just for the night. I needed to see you. Is it okay?" He pulled back his head, his arms kept me close, as if he wasn't ready to let go.

"Of course. I was just surprised. Didn't know you knew how to drive American cars." I grinned and tilted my head toward the car. That was good; I was good. I cracked a joke, so nothing was wrong.

He laughed. "It's an airport loaner. They're fresh out of Bentleys. You eaten?"

I shook my head. "Not yet. You?" I headed toward the house, my right hand digging in my jacket for my keys. I pulled them out with a flourish, spinning to Brett and shaking them. "Look. Locked up and everything."

"God, you're sexy when you're safety-conscious," he growled, his hand catching my waist and pulling me close for a kiss. "And no, I'm starving. Can I treat you to dinner?"

"Dare to try Beverly's again?" I turned the key and shouldered open the door, kicking off my boots and shrugging out of my jacket.

"Absolutely." He stepped in after me and pushed the door shut. There was a moment of eye contact, then Beverly's was forgotten in a strip of clothes and inhibitions.

The next morning I smiled, lifted his bag, and passed it to him.

Kissed him back and laughed when he squeezed my ass.

Waved and smiled until the plane started up and rolled away.

Wondered if the trepidation showed in my eyes.

Questioned, at that moment, if I should just cut bait or walk away.

I cut bait.

chapter 49

As a child, I believed in research. The library was my babysitter, my teacher, my extra friend. Now, six days after the breakfast with my father, with no further information found, the DNA results still pending, I took the pieces I had and dove into the terrifyingly honest world of the Internet.

It didn't take long. I took what I knew: that Brett spent his weekends in Central America and the Caribbean. That he had been questioned in disappearances of girls who ran drugs. That he disappeared late in the night on our trips, had 'boat clients' that didn't exist, hung out in clubs and bars.

I was a small town girl. Knew how to drive a tractor and use my manners. I didn't know, till that horrific Sunday night on my laptop, about the world of drug traffickers.

Google opened my eyes. Taught me everything I didn't want to know and more. I put a TV dinner in the microwave and forged on. Stayed up till two and read until my contacts dried out. I found out that drug traffickers often use women to mule drugs to and from the US. Found out that South Florida has the highest percentage of drug millionaires. Found out that the majority of drug traffickers also deal in illegal arms. One helpful site provided the Top 10 Places Where a Drug-Related Crime is Most Likely to Occur. We, in the last six months of 'romantic' getaways, had hit seven of the spots. I closed my laptop, bolted to the bathroom, and vomited.

Then I threw my untouched Lean Cuisine into the trash and tried to think.

Maybe there was another explanation. Maybe the girls who disappeared, the ones he was questioned about, were innocent tourists. Had nothing to do with drugs at all. Maybe Brett was lying about his real name and job because he didn't want me to know about his wealth. Maybe his late night meetings really were with boat buyers, and he acted as both a manufacturer *and* sales agent. Maybe I was fucking naïve and had fallen in love with a drug-running psychopath.

That night, when Brett called, I didn't answer.

He called me three more times, then Jena called. Said he'd called her and was worried about me living out there alone. Was worried I was in trouble. I told her to let him know I was safe and had gone to bed with a migraine.

Jena didn't ask questions, she repeated the instructions and hung up.

He texted me a few minutes later.

I love you. Hope you feel better soon. Please lock your door.

I turned my phone off and crawled into bed. Let Miller get in, the bed creaking under our weight, and hugged him. Worked my mind through every bit of our vacations, finding red flags I had overlooked at every turn. I fell asleep crying.

chapter 50
Kitten

tight (tīt)
(adj.) closely-matched competitors
"a tight game"

Everything changed after that cock bite, the moment when I left reason behind and became an animal. Suddenly, I couldn't hide it anymore — the hate, the disgust, the vile rise of venom that came whenever the man came towards me.

We battled through Phase Two, every lesson a fight, a push of pain against wills. I refused his questions, and he punished. I refused his advances, and he punished. He gave up on rape, my efforts making the act too physical for him to bother with. I'd like to count that as a victory, but I don't think sex is a motivation of his. Sex was just an item in his notebook to explore, a chapter that needs to be addressed due to its societal importance. He explored, he raped me enough times to ascertain that I - in no way shape or form - was growing attracted or attached to him. The pain... it wasn't a stimulus either. He dished out the punishment methodically and without relish. Mind you, he wasn't wincing over it, there wasn't an empathetic bone in his body when I was on the floor before him screaming. But he didn't get off on it.

What he liked was the mindfuck.

And, in that battle, he was winning.

I couldn't let him win. I would fight until the day that I died.

I closed my eyes and curled into a ball, the bones of my ass tender against the springs of the bed. Listened to the man breathe heavily in the opposite corner of the room, heard the scratch of his pen as he recorded the day's lesson. He really only needed four words. *Man: 0. Kitten: 1.* I gave him nothing. I took everything. Once he was done writing, he would leave. Stand up and give me a parting shot, something to indicate what fun I could expect the next day. But near the end - for a brief moment during recording – I had a moment of quiet. I released a painful sigh and turned my thoughts to Brett.

"Don't go," he lowered his mouth to my neck and kissed the top of my shoulder. "Stay with me forever."

I pushed against his chest, his hand firm, looped together and pinning me to his chest. I laughed softly, the wind whipping my hair, and burrowed into his chest, his body turning to protect me from the ocean breeze. I hugged him back, looking at the house, the outline impressive against the setting sun, the ocean reflected against the back windows. I do love the house. When I first saw it, I'd been blown away. Now, with half of the surfaces inside corrupted by our actions, I felt some small bit of ownership.

"There's plenty of rooms..." he whispered in my ear.

I pushed away enough to look up into his face. "We have plenty of time, Brett. The rest of our lives."

He smiled. "I like that. The rest of our lives. Promise?"

I smirked at him. "Maybe. If you behave."

"I'll behave," he said, pulling me closer. "I promise."

I should have said yes. Moved in that day and never looked back. Shouldn't have planned on plenty of time when I'd barely had any.

"I'm done." The man stood, his chair shoved backward by the motion.

I said nothing, just watched him, my head against the mattress. Waited for whatever barb would come next.

"With everything, I mean. Your training is complete."

That got my attention. I sat up slowly, the motion causing my stomach to roll. Sitting back, my shoulders against the concrete, I said nothing, just stared at him and waited for more. Inside, amid the pain and the nausea, I felt a flutter - half hope, half dread. *Your training is complete.* What did that mean?

"Tomorrow, your diet will change. You've gotten too thin, you need to put some weight back on. Start bathing again. Return a little to the girl you came here as. In five days, if you have improved, I will release you." He nodded, an odd jerky motion, and turned, pushing the chair through the open gate.

"You will release me?" My voice was hoarse, the words wobbled on their way out. Screams had stripped my throat; vomiting made the condition worse.

"Let's see how you look in five days. If you can look normal and speak to me with some semblance of respect, then yes."

Once through the door, he closed the gate and locked me in. Then, without another word, he left.

I stayed in place, my back against the wall, my hand holding my bruised side, for a long time. Then, with nothing to lose, I crawled to the shower.

It'd been so long. So many notebooks filled with his notes, so many lessons and questions and tests. So much pain and fighting.

Could it really be that easy? Would he really let me go?

chapter 51

I decided the next morning, fresh coffee in my system, dried tears and mascara washed off of my cheeks, to break up with Brett. It had to be done. Anything else would be stupid.

If I confronted him, asked him to explain everything to me, he'd deny it. Without a doubt. No drug kingpin would simply fess up. So he'd lie. And I'd have to either play the fool and believe him, or end it then and alert him to my suspicions. And what if he kills me? Decides that the risk of little ole Riley running around is too great? Or... even worse—what if he adds me to his stable? Replaces my kidney with bags of heroine and lugs me back and forth across the border?

No, confronting him was the wrong move.

So... breaking up. I could do it. Invent some lame girly excuse and let him down easy. Spend the rest of my life wondering what really was going on, and what could have been. Let the first man I've ever really loved walk away.

Yeah, that option sucked. Was smarter, but still sucked.

I got in my car and drove to work. Scratched my leg through a hole in my panty hose and checked my phone. The screen still open to his text from this morning.

Good morning love. Call me when you're up and about.

Another one, an hour later.

R we still on for this weekend?

I didn't think I could do it. Couldn't break up with him. But should. Ugh. I had to be the most wishy-washy woman on the planet. I parked my car and walked in the branch, waving to the tellers and unlocking my office. Roses, last week's delivery from Brett, sat dead on the corner of my desk. Already decaying, they filled the room with a slightly sour smell. Dead roses. A fitting touch. And of course, it being Monday...

"Delivery for you." Anita stuck her head in the door.

"Send 'em in," I mumbled, leaning down to press the power button on my computer.

I barely spoke to the delivery boy as he took the dead ones away and replaced them with a new vase - tulips, the cheery yellow flowers doing nothing to brighten my mood. I stopped him on his way out. "Can you take them to Anita instead?"

He stopped, his hand catching the door, head whipping to me. Confusion in the teenager's eyes. "Anita?"

"The blonde manager at the front. Just put them on her desk. I'm fighting allergies this week." I sniffed, rather convincingly.

"Sure. Whatever you want."

"Thanks." I spun in my chair and watched him carry Brett's gift out of my office.

R we still on for this weekend?

I unlocked my phone and returned to the message. This weekend was Puerto Vallarta, a place we'd been before - #11 on the Places Where a Drug-Related Crime is Most Likely to Occur list. Last time, we'd stayed at a bed and breakfast, there'd been a storm, and we'd spent most of the time in bed. Brett had had one meeting - Saturday night - I'd been on my own for dinner and had eaten at the restaurant next door. I'd been so engrossed in my novel I hadn't minded the time apart. Had finished my book five minutes before he had returned, his spirits high. He'd had a car waiting out front, and we'd gone into the city for a late dessert and drinks. I hadn't thought anything about it. Had left my novel in the B&B, but taken my naïveté with me.

I typed without even having a plan, the scent of flowers still heavy in the space.

Are we staying at the same place as before?

The boy was on top of his texts. His response was immediate.

Are you feeling better? Free to talk?

No. In a meeting.

I scrolled back and added a frowny face at the end. Very convincing. I should quit banking and join the CIA. In fact ... I tapped my phone against the desk.

"What's with the flowers?" Anita stuck her head in. "They poisonous?"

"Jury's still out on that," I murmured. I looked up, her eyebrows high, curiosity raised. Shit. Why was I feeding the Quincy rumor mill? I reached for a tissue and pointed toward my nose. "My allergies are hell right now. Any little thing is freaking them out. Do you mind babysitting them till I get over this?"

"Oh... sure. If you need me to fly off to paradise this weekend in your stead, I could do that too."

I smiled big. Tried to laugh but it sounded like a guffaw so I quickly stopped. Maybe my acting wasn't as amazing as I envisioned. "Thanks."

"We have a projections meeting in twenty."

"I'll be there." I fought the urge to stand up, push her out the door, and lock it, so I could finish my thought process. Thankfully, it wasn't necessary. She gave me a cheery wave and left.

I closed my eyes, tried to return to where I was, the buzz of my phone in my hand stopping the act. I looked down at the incoming text.

I thought we'd stay somewhere else this time. Closer to where we had dessert.

So in the city. Near the nightclubs and a gazillion places deals could occur. Maybe I could get my answers without asking the questions. Follow Brett when he disappeared for his "business meeting". Verify my suspicions myself.

I typed a response, the scent of my relationship's blood in the water.

I've got a lot of work stuff to catch up on, not sure I can get away this weekend.

Yeah, that sounded good. Offhand and casual, with no hint of an evil scheme.

Would you prefer me to come to Quincy?

Shit. That wasn't the answer I'd wanted. That type of weekend only worked *before*. Before I knew. Before I suspected. Now, it'd be a disaster. No palm trees or vacation sex to hide my suspicions behind.

My panties were so wet it was embarrassing. I panted against the night air, struggling for silence, the murmurs of the couple that had stepped outside breaking the silence of the night. Was I really being humped in the shadows against the side of a building? Was this beautiful man really running the pad of his fingers back and forth, lower and higher, finding the—oh my god. My head dropped back, and I couldn't stop the moan that escaped me when my silk-covered clit was brushed by his fingers.

Yes, there would have to be at least one more fuck. I needed that. The long stretch of sexual celibacy ahead demanded that. Would I ever meet another man who would make me feel like this? Who would make my back practically break with the strength of my orgasm? Who would bury his face between my legs with such enthusiasm? Caress my body with such worship? Moan my name with such reverence?

Would you mind if I brought the work with me? Maybe I could fit it in at some point?

I threw the lure and waited for him to grab it.

Of course. I'll have a few meetings anyway.

I let out a held breath and looked at the files before me. Moved one aside, looked at the next. All files that couldn't leave this office. Not without jeopardizing my job. I rolled right, pulled open a drawer of my file cabinet. There — reports and reimbursement forms I'd put off for months. They could come. Sit in my suitcase. I could decide in Puerto Vallarta whether to really knock out this busy work... or find out the truth.

CHAPTER 52
BRETT

I looked at our text history. Tried to figure out if I'd done something wrong. Something felt off. We hadn't gone a night without speaking in months. Maybe she'd just - like her friend said - had a migraine. Maybe it was nothing.

I reread the texts. She sounded fine, the words were right... it was my nagging sense of unease that was wrong. Maybe I should respond. Cancel this trip and go to Quincy instead. The trip wasn't more important than her. Than us. She had even replaced Elyse, had grown more crucial than my cause. Maybe I should stop the trips altogether. Settle down and live a normal life with her. But damn, it would be hard. Especially when every trip I saw the faces I rescued. Heard their stories, each one a line to Elyse, an iron in the fight against her death.

For a moment, I compared the two women. Elyse had been auburn, thinner than Riley, taller. But they had the same bright smile, complete with dimples. Same wicked sense of humor. They would have gotten along. They would have been friends. Not that that situation would have ever occurred. Without Elyse, I wouldn't have been at Atlantis. Wouldn't have been in the position to approach Riley in the casino. I would have been back home in Fort Lauderdale. Would never have even known this alternative lifestyle. One of blood money and violence, of redemption and fight, of rescue and rehabilitation. Of Riley. And with that final item, the rest faded.

This weekend was a big sale. An annual event where hundreds of women would be bought and sold. I was expected, women were being brought specifically for my purchase. But I could send one of the guys. Didn't have to physically *be* there for the exchange. But I should be close. I could fly out with Riley. Make sure the guys got into the house and had it ready for the girls. Make sure they had the cash and protection. And I'd work on Riley and our relationship. Make sure that that was in order. Maybe I'd go to the sale. Maybe I'd let the men handle it. I'd play it by ear.

And next week, once the new girls were safely back in the States, I'd examine my life. Make a decision about Riley and stick with it. Either tell her the truth, or kill this part of my life altogether. Abandon the cause. Abandon Elyse's memory to save my future.

I typed a final response to her.

I love you.

Once I sent the text, I stared at those words, ones I never thought, after losing Elyse, that I'd say. I never thought, after her death, I'd be *able* to love, to care, for another individual. Not when I saw what love did. How it exposed a part of your heart for destruction. A part that just lay, vulnerable and exposed, and waited for the pain that would eventually come.

I opened my desk drawer and pulled out the velvet box. Flipped it open and stared at the ring.

I was, with Riley, vulnerable. Open for destruction. But the vulnerability was worth it. I flipped the box shut and returned it to the drawer. The proposal wouldn't happen this weekend. I didn't want that precious moment to come on a weekend of work, in a city where so many lives had been destroyed.

We had a hundred more trips ahead of us. Next week, after I made my decision, after I either told her or left the life, then I'd plan the perfect trip. Maybe to Sydney or Paris. A city where I'd never seen a beaten woman, where I'd never touched a collar or set of cuffs, where I had never traded cash for a human life. A fresh city where we would begin the second half of my life.

I shut the drawer and rolled forward in the chair. Paused in my reach for the mouse and picked up the framed photo of Elyse that sat on the desk. Studied the image, one of the two of us at a twenty-first birthday party, her head thrown back in a laugh, my arm around her shoulders. It was my favorite picture of her, one that perfectly captured her spirit.

"I love you," I murmured, closing my eyes and sending the message upward. "I miss you so fucking much."

Then I opened the drawer and gently set the frame inside, next to the black ring box.

"Boss." The voice made me push the drawer shut, wiping my eye with a brusque hand before turning.

"What's up?" I met the eyes of Joe, my right hand, both here at Betschart Yachts, and in our underground endeavors.

"We're all set for this weekend. House is booked, the travel and security is ready. Jana says we've got room for eight at the house."

"Then we'll get eight." An unnecessary statement, but the man simply nodded.

"Yes sir." He hesitated. "Will you be traveling alone, sir?"

"No. I'll bring Riley. But I'll be on the black cell. And I'll most likely attend the party."

That gave the man pause. "Most likely, sir?" he arched an eyebrow. For Joe, who'd served in four tours of duty before coming to me, it was tantamount to insubordination.

"Yeah. Most likely. If not, you guys can handle it." I turned back to the computer.

Most likely. Probably. I'd have to wait and see.

chapter 53

2 days before

The entire week was a battle to act normal. It was actually easier than I thought. I just allowed the weak feminine part of myself that swooned over every word the man spoke to run lead in my brain. I let her plan weddings on Pinterest during my lunch break, let her gush over his texts, babble to him about her boring day. Hell, on Wednesday, I even let her bring the tulips back from Anita's desk, the woman shooting me a pleading look that *almost* got her them back.

So, I acted the part. And he bought it. And I held my panic and insecurities till late at night, when I'd gorge on peanut butter ice cream and talk Miller's ear off. Flip through every outfit in my closet and lament what to pack. I was going into an impossible situation, knowing *nothing* about when and where to go. I wore the keys on my laptop out, Googling every angle of the Puerto Vallarta drug market I could find. Update: There's nothing to find online. I was hoping for a giant "We Sell Drugs Here" ad, but got nothing. I did discover that taxis swarm our hotel like locusts, so I was able to cross "surveillance vehicle" off the list.

By Thursday, I had a brand new pair of black jeans and a black turtleneck in my suitcase. Bought a pair of low heels that would both fit into a club and allow me to jog with some degree of efficiency. I know, I practiced. Back and forth on my front porch. I could even jump over Miller's body in them if I got a running start. I had withdrawn three hundred dollars in cash, which I figured was enough to get me a cabbie for as long as I needed it, along with extra in case I had to follow Brett inside a club.

I remembered the last club experience, when I had lasted about ten minutes before saying "fuck it". I'd do better this time. I had a reason, it wasn't like before, when I was being nosy and didn't really have a dog in the fight.

My final nights in Quincy, it took me hours to fall asleep. I finally succumbed to the comforting thought that, in Puerto Vallarta, I'd finally have some answers, resolution either way. Soon I'd have enough information to make a decision about whether to walk away from this man.

chapter 54
Kitten

tight (tīt)
(adj.) changing direction abruptly
"a tight turn"

I didn't have a mirror in my cell, but my self-perusal was encouraging. I didn't know how many days have passed, but I'd showered four times. Eaten every bit of food that he had brought. The first day, I vomited half of it up, my stomach unused to the large amount of food. After that I did better, eating smaller meals slower.

My bruises had faded but were still there. My side, a pain that had existed for a while, still flared if I moved in the wrong way. But I'd gained some weight, the poke of my hipbones less pronounced, the line of my veins less noticeable on my arms.

This day felt like it was time: day five. I shook with excitement when he entered. Stayed silent during his examination, the drag and poke of his pen over my nudity. Bit back a hundred questions as he nodded silently.

"Good." He tilted a head to the box, one he had carried in with him, a box I had snuck glances at for the last ten minutes. "New clothes are in the box." He stepped back and nodded permission at me.

I knelt carefully before the box, opening it slowly, savoring the moment. I passed the test. I was getting new clothes. I'd worn, since the day I arrived, the same three pairs of black scrubs, hand-washed occasionally with my shampoo in the shower. I'd imagined a hundred times what had been in that present that I'd kicked through the bars. Something pretty to wear? There were days, during this servitude, that I would've cried over a new outfit. And to think that now, along with freedom, I was getting something new. I bent back the lid and pulled out a few thin plastic packages. A pair of sweatpants, *pink*. A white long-sleeved T-shirt, the material soft and thin. Socks, still in the package. A cheap pair of tennis shoes, a tag on their laces indicating a size too big for me. I blinked at the small pile, my chest tight, tears welling. New clothes, never been worn. Never been bled on, ripped, or ordered off. I wiped at my eyes and carried the pile to my bed. Turned away from him as I dressed. I wanted to thank him. Was more grateful, right then, than I'd ever been my entire life. Grateful, prior to that moment, was a word misused a thousand times. I finished dressing and turned to kneel before him, clasping my hands together, my eyes down. It was the tenth time I'd assumed the subservient position since the day I cracked. The day I crunched onto his cock and didn't let go. The day that turned that cell into a battlefield and painted the walls with my stubborn blood.

"Look at me, Kitten."

I lifted my chin and looked into his eyes. Cold eyes. I learned, long ago, the danger that lay in those eyes, the eyes of a psychopath, one who has no trace of human compassion in his veins.

"I am going to give you one final gift before you leave. Are you listening to me, Kitten?"

Kitten. I hid the wince and nodded. I was listening. I was hanging onto every freaking word. Somewhere, in the threads of those clothes, in the open hang of the gate, there was a catch. One that he would tell me. He wouldn't miss the opportunity for reaction recordkeeping.

"You, right now, are the perfect slave. You are listening, you are responding, you are clean and subservient. You are a slave that will be rewarded, time and time again, for your good behavior. You will lead a happy, healthy life in that role." In his swallow, his preparation for the next sentence, I tried to understand. Where he was going, what he was saying. I couldn't figure it out, couldn't connect the dots. "If you revert to the girl you were a week ago, the fighter — you will live a short life of pain and unhappiness. I believe, in that pretty head of yours, that you are a smart woman. Use that intelligence and choose the right path." He smiled and I searched his eyes, a new tightness in my chest, one that had nothing to fucking do with new pink sweatpants.

"What are you saying? I thought you were letting me go?"

"Oh, I am. I'm done with you Kitten, just as I said. I'm going to let you go to a new home. One with a more experienced Master than I. But you're *not listening*, Kitten." He reached forward, gripping my chin and holding it in place. It was an empty action, my eyes were already stuck on him. "I'm *letting* you pick your home. Your behavior tomorrow night will determine your place. You see, there are two types of women who will be sold. Those trained, and those untrained. The untrained women are whored out, sold to prostitution rings or purchased by sadists looking for entertainment. The trained women are treasured, put up in stables nicer than my home and spoiled rotten. I'll be buying a trained girl, one who will actually be helpful in my research. I know that you can play the part, Kitten. Be the good little slave long enough to get a good home. Then, who knows? Maybe you'll be smart enough to stay that way. Maybe seeing both worlds will give you the push to submit that I never could."

I am ashamed to say, with his hand hard on my chin, that I cried. Right there, big crocodile tears pouring down my cheeks, I blubbered like a weak child. Begged him to let me go. Promised him that I would never tell anyone, that I would pay him anything. I cried and gripped his forearms and reached for the buckle of his pants. Offered up my body, my thoughts, everything in exchange for freedom.

I twisted away when I felt the prick of the needle. A familiar feeling... like the night that he took me. This time, instead of falling into his arms, I fell back, onto the cardboard box, his face hovering above me before my world went black.

I was negotiating with all of the wrong things. He didn't want anything more to do with me. He wanted a new slave.

chapter 55

It's easy, with Brett, to forget. About the two drug mules who disappeared, about the false identity, about my suspicions. It's easy to forget when his smile made my heart swoon. When he wrapped his arms around me and I couldn't help but laugh. I should have stayed in Quincy. I didn't realize that my resolve had no chance in his presence.

He hung an arm around my shoulders as we walked from the plane. I glanced around the airport, at the lines of planes hitched to the concrete, the lot's lights illuminating the row against the black night sky. Tuesday, I had enlisted Jena. Didn't give her details, just told her Brett's real name and had her sit down with me, show me the sites she uses when she snoops. The woman can't parallel park, but she's lethal in investigation when given the proper tools. I didn't want to give her the proper tools, didn't want to share my suspicions with the largest mouth in Gadsden County. So she snooped, I watched, and within fifteen minutes, the Internet revealed that Betschart Yachts owned two planes. One, the Navajo Chieftain that we'd always used. The other? A Citation jet, one that could seat twelve and make the jaunt from Quincy to Puerto Vallarta in forty-five minutes. Our flight had taken almost two hours.

"So... maybe he's cheap. It's cheaper to fly the Chieftain, right?"

Jena slow-blinked at me in response across the kitchen table.

"Or..." I muttered defiantly, "maybe he just *prefers* it."

She shrugged. "Sure. Except..." she spun the laptop towards me and tapped one acrylic nail on the top of the screen. "Here's the last six months' worth of flights that the Citation's taken."

"How'd you find this?" I scooted closer.

"FAA flight plans are public record. Notice anything interesting?"

I somehow heard the pop of her gum over the loud thud of my heart. I sat back, turning this information over in my head. "Yeah. It's gone to all of the same places we went."

"And on the *same days*," Jena trumpeted. "Now," she leaned back and crossed her arms, scrunching her face in textbook perplexity, "what the hell is up with that?"

I feigned confusion. Did a lot of shoulder shrugs and gasps of disbelief. Then all but pushed her out the door in an attempt to hide my poor acting. It doesn't make sense to bring two planes. Not unless you wanted to bring back to the States something you didn't want your girlfriend to find out about. Now, on Puerto Vallarta's airstrip, I looked for the Citation, searched for its tail number among the line of vehicles.

"Wanting to swap planes?" Brett teased, his arm tightening around me, pulling my head to his mouth.

I shook my head. "No, just looking. I didn't realize how many different types of planes there are. Have you ever thought about getting another?"

Awesome segue. Maybe I did have a future in stealth. I looked away from the planes and towards the customs office. I hadn't seen it. Maybe Jena's information was wrong.

"No, the Chieftain handles my needs just fine. Plus, it'll land anywhere in anything. Bigger planes cause more problems."

I searched for a hidden, drug-related meaning in his words, but came up blank.

chapter 56
Kitten

I woke up, at some point, confined, the hum of a car putting me - most likely - in a trunk, tape obstructing my mouth and eyes from any further information gathering. There was something hard against my back, each bump in the road throwing me against it. I tried to roll, tried to bend, the metal cuffs around my wrists and ankles keeping me in place, the only result a jarring knock on the head when I tipped forward. I stayed still, tried to listen, tried to think.

It was hot in there. I wondered how long I had been unconscious, my T-shirt stuck to my back, the sweatpants claustrophobic in their heavy nape.

A line of sweat trailed down my back. I listened hard, but heard nothing.

chapter 57

Brett won't fuck up. He's being perfect, attentive at dinner, thoughtful at dessert, his typical dominant sex-god-self when we shut the door and are alone in the room. And at 1 AM, when I couldn't sleep - he rolled over and began rubbing my back. A slow trail of fingers across the bare skin, feather light, the scrape of occasional nails just enough to keep the skin from getting itchy.

I swallowed. "I have *got* to get to that work tomorrow."

"That's fine, just let me know when you want to work on it."

I kicked a foot out from underneath the covers. Let the cool air hit it. "It doesn't really matter. Do you have meetings tomorrow?"

His hand never paused in its delicate journey over my skin. "I don't need to go, we can do whatever you want."

Don't need to go? I frowned. Not that I wanted to encourage drug-running, but didn't the main guy have to be present at these things? And this was my weekend to figure this out, to step closer to this man or break everything off. A decision I couldn't make if he changed his entire MO this trip.

"No, please." I forced a playful lilt into my words. "*Please* get out of my hair for a few hours and let me knock this stuff out. I can get room service for dinner and call you when I'm done."

"I don't want to abandon you this weekend. Are you sure?" His voice was closer, his hand moving around my side, the settle of his body against my back so perfect that I sighed, looping my fingers through his and holding them to my chest.

"I'm sure. Trust me."

Trust me. Part of me wished he did. The other part of me was grateful he didn't.

chapter 58
Kitten

Tonight, I will be sold. I repeated the line over and over again. I would not be rescued, I would not escape. I would be sold and become the property of a new man. And the chances of freedom would be further reduced.

As much as I hate to say it, He was right. I would, if I presented myself correctly, be more valuable to buyers. And I had to imagine that, the more a buyer paid, the higher the investment, the better I would be treated. And vice versa - the more worthless I was, the less kindness and care I could expect to receive.

So... I should behave. Act subservient, act broken. Become valuable. Sell for a high price and invest in my future. Pray for the type of owner who is kind to his sex slaves. An impossible prayer yet I whispered it anyway.

Tonight, I will be sold.

Turns out repetition of the phrase doesn't make it any less painful.

***

Tonight I would get answers.

Everything started to fall into place around nine, after a long dinner, then drinks. My foot jiggled under the table, I barely touched the food, and I checked my watch so many times that Brett signaled for the check. "I'm sorry babe. Do you need to get to that work? They can cork the wine."

I glanced at the wine, freshly opened, a bottle worth more than my car, and hated to nod, hated to throw away the wine - and the moment - of which there'd, most likely, never be another. I nodded. "I'm sorry."

He grinned. "Don't be. I hate to see you stress. And I'll be drinking all night with the clients. It'll be better if I stop now. Keep my wits about me."

I returned the smile and studied the lines of his face, the loose freedom of his posture, the compliment he gave the waiter as he scribbled a generous tip on the bill. I just didn't see it. Maybe I was blinded by love but I couldn't picture Brett engaged in an illegal drug ring. Or arms trafficking. Or questioned over missing drug mules. Despite the red flags, despite all the evidence to the contrary, he *felt* innocent.

Or was it just that I didn't *want* to see the truth? Was I just so blinded by love and the *thought* of love that I washed over anything to the contrary? I watched Brett shake the waiter's hand and stand, pulling out my chair.

Can't be. No way.

We walked back to the room, he stole a kiss in the elevators, pinning me against the wall. "Time for a quickie before your work?"

Not this man. Not Brett. Anyone else.

"I can't baby. But when you get back," I promised, smiling at the glaze of his eyes, a glaze of arousal that wouldn't wait till later, a hypothesis proved when he lifted me over his shoulder and carried me to our room, tossing me on the bed, his fingers quick, cock ready, the access of my dress making his first thrust easy and incredible.

I am wrong. I will prove it tonight. I will follow him, and watch him sell a boat. Woo a perfectly legitimate client. Be the man that I desperately want to believe that he truly is.

I rolled off of him, moving to the bathroom, running the shower before unzipping my dress and stepping in. "That's not fair," he groaned from his place in the doorway, his hands busy at his cuffs, the rest of him in perfect place except for his hair. I watched him pull on his jacket and shot him a grin, stepping into the shower and wiggling my fingers at him. "Go. Sell your little boats."

I kept my hair out of the spray and ran a bar of soap quickly over me. Wasn't the slightest bit surprised when the door opened and Brett's hand stole in, caressed the soap bubbles on the closest breast.

"I can't leave you without a kiss."

I stepped forward, rinsed the soap off and turned the knob. Waved off the steam and stepped out, into the fluffy towel that he held open. Blushed as he wrapped the terrycloth around and rubbed me down, lingering over his favorite places and finishing the process by tugging at my hair tie, his eyes smiling as my curls bounced free, his mouth coming down soft and sweet on my own. I smiled against his mouth. "Happy? You got your kiss."

He stole another. "Completely," he whispered.

I am mistaken. There is nothing wrong with this man.

I heard the door click behind him, and sprang into action.

chapter 59

I had a secret weapon in my pursuit of Brett: My iPod Touch, a mini MP3 player that had one awesome feature - the ability to be found via the Find a Phone app. I slipped the iPod into his jacket before sex. Watched him walk out the door and I pulled up the app. Checked his location *the lobby* while jerking on my black jeans, tight sweater and superhero boots. I left my hair down - then, remembering Brett's eyes on my curls, the fascination he had with their bounce - I twisted it into a low knot. Stuck a room key in my pocket and jogged down the hall and back to the rear stairwell. Thank God we were on the fourth floor and not the twenty-fourth. I hit the ground floor running and burst out the side, coming out in the loading zone, a flash of yellow taxis visible around the side of the building.

More jogging, the low heel of the boots thudding across the empty space, the last taxi in line spotting me early and jerking into reverse, skidding its way into a tight U-turn and pulling up to the side curb.

"Please pull through the front," I called out to the man, slumping down in the seat. "I want to see if my friend's out front."

He nodded as if he understood and pulled another U-turn. Bounced into the portico and slowed down. Too slow. If Brett was standing there he'd be... my app refreshed, Brett's dot on the screen moving, and I saw him ahead, on the curb, speaking with a group of men.

Thank God. His clients. I let my head fall back against the seat. I was crazy, he was innocent. I opened my purse, ready to pull out some cash and let the cabbie go when one of the men turned my way and I saw his face. *Shit.* I ducked in the car. "Pull out," I said urgently. "Anywhere. Just move."

I had seen the man before. In Brett's house in Fort Lauderdale, huddled, like they are now, around Brett. Four men, the same four men. Brett's 'friends.'

I told the cabbie to pull over and park. I spun in the seat, watched Brett's foursome, and waited. It didn't take long. A line of three black SUVs pulled up tight to the curb, the men all piling into the first one. Then, the convoy moved, a pack of shiny black, pulling off the curb and onto the street. "There." I pointed when they passed us. "Follow them."

I shouldn't have followed them. I should have paid the cabbie, gotten out, and walked back into the lobby. Taken the elevator up to my room and waited for Brett. You see, here is where my story ends.

chapter 60
Kitten

My new cell was a motel room, one on the end, with windows that didn't open and a rotten smell that wouldn't stop. I felt dawn when we arrived, saw bits of light along the edge of my blindfold. He dragged me backwards by my cuffs into the ground floor room, my blind feet tripping over the curb, my entrance inside made in a clumsy heap of restrained limbs.

He lifted me onto a bed and I slept for some time, the mattress so soft compared to the trunk, compared to my cell's mattress. I woke when he ripped the tape off. The handcuffs were removed next, and I rolled my ankles and wrists for a while before walking to the bathroom.

It had been so long since I'd looked in a mirror that I'd forgotten what I looked like. I leaned forward and gingerly touched my cheeks. Saw the stranger before me do the same. The stranger with the faded black eye. The stranger who looked stronger than I ever did. Who stood straight and glared into the mirror and dared me to criticize her scars. I stepped back. Used the restroom, washed my hands with the bar soap, then glanced at him. Got permission and opened the makeup bag that sat on the counter with trembling fingers.

I pulled out the contents and lined them up, in a neat row on the counter.

Revlon Photoready 3D Volume Mascara: Black
Maybelline Instant Age Rewind Eraser Concealer: Light
Revlon ColorStay Pressed Powder: Light/Medium
Revlon Super Lustrous Lipstick: #680 Temptress

The wrong colors for me, but I didn't care. They were used cosmetics, which bothered me more. Who had they belonged to? Where had they come from?

"It would be in your best interest to look nice." He spoke from the doorway, a few steps away, and watched me. I wished for a door between us, some privacy in this moment. I reached for the concealer, applied it generously, painting the bruises white, the black eye pale. I used every trick my mother had ever taught me. Took my time with my brows, applied mascara with a shaky hand and lined my lips carefully before applying the color. Finger-combed through my hair and wished for a curler, something to tame the wild mess it had become.

Then, I laughed. I couldn't help myself, the sound bubbled out of me, as foreign in my throat as his cock. What was I *doing*? Why was I *trying*? I wanted a *curler*? There I was, hours from being sold, and I was worried about my looks. About making a good impression. I stared at my reflection and had the sudden desire to slam my head forward, into the glass. Had a mild moment of pleasure at the idea of him trying to sell me then, a bloody-faced girl with glass in her hair.

Instead I turned, like a good little slave, and faced him.

"What am I going to wear?"

"There's a dress hanging in the closet." He touched the edge of my elbow as I passed, my entire body jerking to a stop at the contact. "You look very nice," he said quietly.

"Thank you, sir." I intoned, my head down.

The dress was plain, a short black number, Ross tags still attached. I slid it on and stepped in front of the mirror.

"Perfect," he murmured from behind me, his eyes critiquing every inch of the look, his hand tucking in the tags, smoothing out the fabric.

I kept my eyes down and forced a smile.

***

I don't think that there has ever been a moment in my life where I knew, with absolute certainty, that my entire life was about to change. I didn't realize it the night I was abducted. Didn't realize it, as a baby, the night of my birth. But this night, I knew it. I knew that every action I took would have some form of consequences for the rest of my life. One wrong glance, one misstep... and it could end in death, or worse - a lifetime of torture.

I broke every rule I'd ever made for myself and cooperated. Let him cuff my hands. Stepped from the room and through the parking lot and didn't scream. Saw my first sky in unknown years and stared. Took a seat in the front seat of a car I had never seen next to a man that I wanted dead. Quietly sat while he drove me through a city whose name I didn't know. The car stopped, started, accelerated, slowed. Turned twenty-odd times before pulling down a street and stopping.

I'd been down streets like this before. Cobblestoned paths that led between buildings centuries old. I walked down a street like this with Brett before. He bought a flower from a street kid and tucked it in my hair. Pulled me into an alley and kissed my mouth, put his hand up my dress and caressed my thigh.

I shouldn't have thought of Brett. The man who used to give me strength—just that slight thought of him broke my veneer. Made my hands shake and my stomach twist. I always thought, in the confines of that basement, that he would find me. Now, hours from that home, in a city I didn't recognize, where I would be sold to a real Master, not some psychotic slave researcher... he'd never find me. Not him, not my father, not the police. I would be lost, I would be a statistic, like so many I had heard about over the course of my training.

The car settled into park and I looked at my hands. Felt the brush of his palm on my bare shoulder and fought the urge to recoil.

"I've been very impressed with you, Kitten. Maybe you *are* smart enough to keep this up."

I wished he would just shut up. Find a bridge in this country and jump off of it. I stared at my hands and waited for him to come around, open my door, lead me to slaughter.

When we entered the room we were greeted by a voice. I stared at the shoes of the man speaking, shiny and perfect, and wondered if he had a wife who polished them. Polished them and straightened his tie, kissing his cheek before waving goodbye. I wondered if this man beat her or if he treated her like a queen. I wondered, not for the first time, at whether my keeper had someone, a wife or girlfriend who he feigned affection and forced smiles for. I wondered if he carried around a clipboard and bugged *her* with questions all day.

"There are fifteen buyers here tonight. The rest of the group is in the main room. You only brought her?"

"Yes. And I'm also looking to purchase." I could hear the eagerness in his voice, a nerd wanting to sit at the cool kids' table.

"Oh." Polished Shoes shifted. *Ha.* I smiled to myself. He heard it too. "Have you been here before?"

"A while ago. We spoke then. I'm surprised you don't remember."

"Then you already know the house rules. Please wear these two pins, they'll indicate that you are both buying and selling. I suggest you make Buyer 43's acquaintance. He's always looking for American girls to purchase, though he typically breaks them himself."

"He's here? I've heard his name before." I could practically hear him quiver with excitement. This was it. What his months of research, his stacks of journals had led to. I hadn't had a chance, begging for my life a few days earlier. This was a moment he'd been waiting for, planning for, for a very long time. I'd just been the stupid girl who had given him a key to the city.

"He rarely misses a sale."

"Well, let's go in." He put pressure on my arm and I stepped forward, following his lead, the two of us following the shiny shoes through the doors.

In the entryway, my head down, listening to the conversation of my keeper and the greeter, I wanted to raise my head, look around. See what I was walking into. But, stepping down a wide hall, I suddenly didn't want to look. Didn't want to know. Heard, before us, screams of women, cries of terror and desperation. I slowed my steps, felt his hand close on my wrist and tighten. A warning.

My steps increased in speed, my chest hammering as I blew a shaky breath out. Tonight, I would be sold. The further we went, the more my ears understood. There were two groups of sound before us, a division of order and chaos, and when the hall ended, I tilted my head right, raising my eyes enough to see a hallway, the screams of women coming from that direction. To my right, a quiet hum mixed with delicate strands of music.

"Kitten, look at me."

I lifted my eyes, then my chin, looking into his face.

"Can I trust you to make the right choice?" He held up a handcuff key. Moved his gaze right, then left. "I can take you either place. Two different groups of buyers. It's up to you."

I swallowed. Fought the urge to glance right, one woman's long howl cutting a path through my composure. I held up my wrists. "I will be good, Master. I promise."

He smiled. Worked the cuff's lock open as I dropped my gaze. I saw his hand, long fingers that have yanked my hair, slapped my face, violated me...slip the cuffs into the pants pocket of his suit. A suit. I missed that detail, too absorbed in my own fate. Is that the proper outfit to wear when shopping for a soul?

"Ready, Buyer 214?" Polished Shoes had moved left, to the door.

"Please. Lead the way."

When the door opened, it brought with it the smell.

chapter 61
Kitten

tight (tīt)
(adj.) very firm so as not to let go
"a tight grip"

The smell was of men, a raw animal scent of domination and want. Of competition, them all just a few steps short of beating their chests and howling. We stepped forward, my hands clasped together, head down, the room a quiet roar of conversation, male voices stacked upon male voices, in the background, the clink of metal and glassware, small bits of feminine voices sprinkled in. I listened for screams, but heard none. Relaxed slightly and felt his hand on my back, guiding me through the crowds. Saw Polished Shoes' departure, the handshake that passed between the two vultures, a bit of cash exchanged in the clasp.

"Would you like a drink?" his voice was low and nervous, and I watched the tic of his hand, fluttering against his coat pocket, as if unsure whether to go in or out of the space.

"No thank you, Master." I could be good. I could behave. Maybe we could go back to Phase One, this time with my cooperation. My life, in Phase One, had been a bearable one.

I felt the stiffening before I saw it, the switch that flipped and knew, even before the shoes came into view, that we were being approached. A single set of men's dark brown dress shoes. A buyer.

"She looks American." I searched for a hint in the man's voice, an accent, an inflection, but got nothing from those words.

"She is. And well-trained."

"Fully broken?"

"Yes."

"She looks rough, like she's been punished recently."

There was a pause before he spoke, a moment where I felt a ridiculous moment of hurt, the criticism stinging. I had never been described as 'rough.' Never considered, in the hours leading up to this, the possibility that I might not be wanted.

He finally spoke. "Not a punishment. Just my form of sex." He laughed, an awkward bark, and the man stepped back.

"Not my thing. Good luck."

Not my thing. I wanted to call out, *Wait! It's not my thing either! We'd be perfect together!* Instead, I watched his shoes move a few steps over, heard his greet of another couple. Cheated a bit and lifted my eyes to the right. Saw shoes and slacks and bare legs displayed on heels. People everywhere.

"Keep your eyes down," he hissed. "And try to look fucking pleasant."

Pleasant? I weighed, for a brief moment, the downfalls associated with a swift pivot left and a strong knee to the balls. The thought brought a small smile. Then a strange hand, one that curved around my waist and pinched my skin, so hard and sharp that I wheezed in a breath of protest, stopped that smile.

"Nice... very nice." The stranger hissed when he spoke, his body a stench of alcohol and cologne, my nose getting a front seat to the party when he pulled me closer, against his chest, his thick features rolling into place as he smacked thick lips together and squinted at me from inches away. I dropped my eyes, said nothing, *did* nothing, even as his hand traveled down my back and possessively squeezed my ass.

"How much?"

Not this man, not this man. I'd take a thousand clipboard questions and beg for my keeper's touch before I served this man.

"Fifteen thousand."

Fifteen thousand? I almost lifted my head, almost broke character and stared at my keeper. *That* is all I was worth? That is what the training and hell was for? To increase my value to the point to where my skin fetched the price of a *used fucking* Camry?

"That's too much," the man drawled, his fingers moving across my ass cheeks and digging into the crack. I bit the inside of my cheek and struggled not to speak.

"Twelve." My Master spoke too quickly and I wanted to scream. Twelve thousand??! I had twelve thousand in my savings account at home. Was fairly certain that Brett would pay a hundred times that amount without hesitation. This could *not* be my ending. I wouldn't let it happen.

I raised my head and stared into the man's eyes, the action unexpected, his eyes narrowing in response. Then I licked my Revlon Super Lustrous #680 Temptress lips and spoke.

"Get your fucking hands off of me or so help me God I will break every one of your fingers."

Beside me, my keeper jerked into action, his hand clamping down on my arm harder than I'd ever felt it, the punishment in the bite of every single finger. I fought it, stared into the man's eyes and let him see every ounce of hatred in my heart.

Behind us, a voice, so low and deep that it stopped us all, the casual authority a hundred levels above the three of us.

"Is there a problem here?"

Five words that gripped my heart and smashed it into place.

Five words spoken in a manner I'd never heard yet instantly recognized.

Five words that caused both men to turn but I stayed in place, a tremble starting from my feet and rocketing up, till I thought I'd drop, till I thought, right there on that floor, that I would burst into a hundred pieces.

Brett had found me. I pressed my lips together and fought the breakage of my soul, my eyes squeezing together, a lump in my throat fighting to burst through every opening in my soul.

I had been saved.

chapter 62

The trio of black SUVs were ahead of us, my app verifying Brett's location in the car.

"Very James Bond," the driver called out cheerfully, lifting his chin and meeting my gaze in the rearview mirror.

"Uh-huh." I gripped the front passenger headrest and stared at the cars. Watched as we wound through downtown. Brett's 'friends', the men from the house, now here, with two extra SUVs, headed into the heart of the city. Not going on a boat sales call, that was for certain. They must work for him, be part of the drug operation. I wondered at his house, at all of the rooms that we had passed through, made love in. How many of those rooms had closets full of drugs? Or guns? Or both? How many nights had I sat in a hotel room while he had destroyed lives? Broken a hundred laws? Empowered terrorist and drug organizations?

I had seen enough. I should go back to the hotel. Book a flight home and be halfway to the airport by the time Brett returned.

"You getting out now?"

I raised my head, looked around, scrambling into action when I realized that the brigade before us had stopped, doors opening on all three vehicles, two men I didn't recognize joining Brett's foursome. I glanced at the meter and pulled out a twenty, holding it out. "Keep the change. What is this place?"

He twisted in his seat, taking the cash with an appreciative nod. "A salsa club. Real popular with the tourists. But it's early, won't be too crazy right now. It'll heat up in an hour or so, be really crazy then. Want me to wait for you?"

I glanced around, Brett's entourage entering through the front, the street quiet and relatively clean. "No, I think I'm okay. Taxis come through here often?"

"Oh yes, every few minutes. But here's my card. If you can't find one, just give me a call." He smiled, half his grin void of teeth.

I took the card. "Thanks."

I was slow to exit, a group of girls approaching the club, and I waited for them to pass before stepping out. I followed them closely, an attempt to hide, a barrage of Spanish bouncing between them as they pulled open the doors and shouted a chorus of welcomes to the doorman.

They were my shield, camouflaging my entrance, and my eyes darted around the dim interior quickly, worried that I would turn around and bump into Brett's chest.

I had nothing and everything to worry about. The group of men wasn't there.

I paid the doorman, and hugged the shadows, checking the room once, twice, three times. I visited the restrooms, put my ear to the men's room door, wandered behind the bandstand and out to the patio. The cabby was right, the place wasn't busy, nothing like the moshpit of the Jamaican club.

"Looking for someone?" The man's voice made me jump, my nerves fried, and I spun around, gripping my elbow with a wince when it connected solidly with the edge of a table.

"No, not really." I tried to smile, shook out the arm.

"You just look lost." He stepped back, giving me space, and I relaxed a bit. Took in his dark polo and khakis.

"You work here?"

He shrugged. "You could call it that. I own the club. My name's Mitchell." He extended a hand.

"Riley." I smiled. "Is there more to it? It seems bigger from the outside."

He glanced left, in the direction of a door marked Private. "There's an upstairs, but it's closed to a private party."

Closed to a private party. I rubbed my elbow, my arm tingling from the hit. "You know what kind of party it is?" I should give up. Take a seat in the corner and wait for them to leave, or get out of here.

He grinned. "I could get you in if you are interested."

Am I interested? No. Probably not. Chances are he'll open the door and it'll be a flashback to my experience at Brett's home office, staring blankly at a group of men with no logical purpose for my presence. "No. I was just curious."

"Why don't you come up to VIP? It has a view of the upstairs, plus one of the city."

VIP? I hadn't seen a VIP in my cruise of the club. Then again, I hadn't seen the stairway upstairs but Brett and his cronies had gone *somewhere.* "Are there other people in VIP?"

He laughed. "Where do you think everyone is? There's a reason it's a ghost town down here."

I watched him laugh, the easy tilt of his head, the relaxed sag of his shoulders, the nod he gave to a waitress when she passed.

He was nice. Helpful. A little flirtatious, but that was fine. Trustworthy. Connected. And he could give me a glimpse of the upstairs party.

I   smiled.   "Sounds   good."

chapter 63
Kitten

The five fingers of Him burned into my arm, the twist of his body to look at Brett causing a rug-burn effect, but I stayed in place, my back to him. I couldn't turn, couldn't look into Brett's eyes because if I did... God, if I saw his face my barely controlled emotions would flood. I would sob his name, throw my arms out and fly into his chest. I would grip his shirt, smell his cologne and never let go - they'd have to cut out our chests and separate the beating of our hearts.

"No problem. Just a little negotiation over price. The slave stepped out of place." He jerked with his hand on my arm and I stumbled around, into my keeper, my eyes glued to the floor, the wet brim of tears threatening to fall as I did everything to stop myself from looking up.

Brett's shoes. Black dress shoes, the laces tight and neat. If I pulled up his dress pants, I'd see dark silk socks.

He watched me, a playful gleam in his eyes as he pulled his shoes, then his socks off, stretching the black fabric between his hands and standing. Walking to the foot of the bed, he grabbed my ankles and pulled me to the edge, winking at me before he pinned them together and secured them with the silk. "What are you going to do?" I breathed, testing the bind, his weight settling on the bed as he moved against me and propped my bound legs against his shoulder.

"Just wait," he ordered, his hands busy unbuckling his belt.

"The negotiation is over." Brett's voice was quiet yet carried, and I counted the shoes around him. Three other pairs, all pointed this way. I wondered about the men attached to them, if they were ones

I'd met before. Wondered how much of his life that I had misunderstood had revolved around this.

"Actually," the fat man beside me spoke, stepped forward a bit. "It's not. But you're welcome to enter the deal. I might be persuaded to sell my option."

In the silence that followed, I pictured Brett's face, the way his jaw clenched when he held back anger, the way his eyes blazed with authority. When his words finally came, I heard the pent-up bite in their tones.

"Do you know who I am?"

It was an odd response and I stopped counting shoes and remembering and holding back tears, stopped everything to listen. My keeper spoke. "I'd guess, from the room's sudden silence, that you're Buyer 43."

He was right, the room *was* quiet. The hum of masculinity, the laughs and murmurs and feminine chimes - all had stopped. There was nothing more interesting in this space than us. Buyer 43. I tried to remember what had been said.

"...I suggest you make Buyer 43's acquaintance. He's always looking for American girls to purchase, though he typically breaks them himself."

"He's here? I've heard his name before."

"He rarely misses a sale."

I shifted. Returned my gaze to Brett's shoes. Waited for his response. *Always looking for American girls...* he has been looking for me.

"That is correct. This one... she's American?"

"Yes, and well-trained." My keeper practically chirped the response. I stared at my own feet, the cheap heels on them. The type of heels I wore when I met Brett. Not the kind he deserved. *I am well-trained.*

"What price are you thinking?" The fat man put a hand on my shoulder, his fingers spreading and squeezing the skin, leaving a moist print I would probably never fully scrub off. *He almost bought me.*

"I'm thinking that you get your hand off of her and step a*fucking*way before I cut off that hand myself."

The hand left, so did the man. I could almost feel the brush of air as he found his common sense and left.

My Master's words practically jump out, a rush of run-on syllables that melded together into a string of pathetic. "I'm a big fan of yours. Heard about you for years. I'm glad we got the chance to meet, it was really more than I expected, you being here tonight—"

"What is it that you respect?" Brett said coolly. "My purchasing habits? My stable?"

"*Everything.* I'd love to see your facility. Watch you train. I heard you take all types."

"My hobby is not a theme park. You can't come and wander around, eat fucking popcorn and watch me work the girls."

He straightens, shifts in response, and I feel the cold possessive slide of his hand, down the back of my arm and around my waist. "It was nice to meet you. A big honor." He pulled on my waist, moving me a step towards him, the hurt kid taking his toys and going home.

"The band on your arm indicates you're here to buy." Brett's voice interrupts our exit.

"I am."

"You know I have hundreds. Tell me what you are interested in. Or, since you have such an interest in my dealings, come and pick one out."

A slight release, the turn of Him back to Brett. "And what about her?" He tips his head toward me. "You like American girls. Do you want to do a trade?"

"I'll give you twenty for the girl now. You can use it to rebuy tonight, or save it for your trip to my ranch."

I was so close to freedom. I wish I could pin my eyes in place, the danger of them lifting so strong. Brett sounded so calm, so smooth. Was playing the game better than I ever would have been able to.

"Twenty-five?" I may faint if this negotiation lasts much longer.

"No." Brett's voice was cold. "Take the deal or get the fuck out of my sight."

The man beside me laughed, high and awkwardly, his step passing in front of my line of vision, my gaze lifting slightly to see their hands shake. "We have a deal. Enjoy her."

I feel the push of my keeper's *ex-keeper's* hand and step forward. I can't lift my eyes or I will break, am stepping over the edge to freedom, cannot lose this now.

"Come here." It is not Brett who speaks, it's the man on his left, who holds out his hand, and I step towards him, my hands clasped, daring to raise my head and I meet his gaze. It is strong and steady, a hard jaw, kind eyes — I know this man. Met him at Brett's house, the full introduction made in the outdoor kitchen, him setting down tongs long enough to shake my hand and give me his name. I can't remember it, but know that he had two kids, one who played soccer.

He smiled at me but I was too scared to respond. Wanted to be out of this party as soon as possible. Wanted to scrub my skin until I removed every layer of him. Wanted to be alone with Brett and burrow into his chest. Look into his face and rediscover every detail I'd struggled to memorize. Never let go of him.

I heard the slap of a handshake behind me, money exchanged, a string of subservient words pouring at Brett from the man who had demanded obedience from me. Heard, or imagined, the click of his shoe as he stepped away. Felt the close of a hand, Brett's hand, around my arm as he gently pushed me forward, steering me toward the door, his voice low and urgent when he turned to the others. "Make sure we get to the car safely, then stay here and deal with the other girls. I'll meet you back at the house."

It took a thousand steps to reach the street, his hand firmly wrapped around my bare bicep, every bit of my skin obsessed with the warm grip of him. A thousand steps where, at one moment, turning a corner, he leaned down and pressed a kiss on the top of my shoulder. Inhaled a deep breath and smelled me. Moved the thumb of his hand gently and caressed the underside of my arm for one moment before we rounded the edge and he was, again, pure business.

When we stepped past Polished Shoes, I took in a shuddering breath. When a hand pushed on the door and it opened, a burst of free air greeting us, the night outside quiet, an SUV ahead of us waiting, the back door opened by a faceless man, I exhaled. Stepped up, into the warm vehicle, the driver turned in his seat, his face flinching in surprise when our eyes connected, recognition hitting us both at the same time. Another meeting. Another time. Another friend.

The door shut behind Brett, the truck accelerated away from the house, and I felt the crush of his arms around me.

He gripped me as if he was drowning, his arms wrapping around me, his head in my neck, breath gasping as if he was broken, a quivering sob of wracking inhalations, the action paused only by his kisses, quick and soft against my shoulder, collarbone, neck. He moved a shaky hand to either side of my face and held it, still, his lips pressing to mine before he pulled away and I looked fully into his face for the first time in the rest of my life. Saw heartbreak there that rivaled my own. Need and stress, a man aged in my time away, his fingers trembling as he ran the pads of digits across my lips.

"I thought..." he shuddered out a breath. "I thought you were gone. Oh my god..." he sobbed, a wet shaky inhale, his hands sliding into my curls and gripping them, pulling me closer.

I dug my hands into his hair and pulled him toward me, our lips meeting and knew in that moment that nothing between us - not with the time, or the separation, or my servitude - had changed. He didn't see me as ruined or used, he gripped me like I was priceless, kissed me like he'd never let go. He was still mine. We were still us.

chapter 64

Whatever he had injected me with, I had my senses about me when he lifted my arm. Threw it over his shoulder and propped me up on my feet. Walked us both past the bathrooms, through the dim hall and back into the club, the floor more crowded, a colorful swirl before me. I tried to reach out a hand, to grab a person, tried to open my mouth and scream for help. Tried to do something other than close my eyes and slump against him.

I heard his laugh, heard words I couldn't understand, saw the door open, the night dark, *my taxi, where was my taxi?* I twisted a floppy ankle on the cobblestone streets, pulled against him and felt his hand tighten, to a point of pain.

This was bad. I tried to yell for Brett, tried to lift my head and look up, to the VIP... *private party* ... and I wondered, for a minute, through the haze, if he was like Brett - a drug trafficker. Maybe I would be a mule, maybe I would...

He threw me in the back seat of a car and shut the door, the hard motion slamming at the bottom of my heel, my knee popping up, my face against a cold vinyl seat. I tried to finish my thought, tried to move my mouth to ask a question tried to... couldn't ....

BLACK.

chapter 65
Kitten

"Oh my god, I thought you were gone." Brett pulled his lips off of mine long enough to whisper the words, the press of his lips against my forehead warm and soft and him. I would never again have to be in that cell. I would never again have to look into that man's eyes or feel his fists or answer his questions. I was no longer a slave, I was free. My mind choked on that final concept and I pulled away, his eyes widening, his pursuit of me halted as he held himself back. I pulled at the neck of the cheap dress, it choking me, the scratch of its polyester against my bare skin hot and lingering and maddening.

"I have to get this off," I blurted out, craning my body, trying to reach for a zipper, the act ripping a hole through my awareness, the pain in my side flaring for one searing moment. "Ow!" Sudden tears, they gave me no warning, just came, a drip of them down my cheek as my hands grew frantic, trying to unzip something that some sadist designed just out of reach.

"Here." His hands soft but efficient, the relieving sound of the zipper, the loosening of the dress and I yanked at it, freeing my upper half, Brett's quick move off the seat shedding his jacket, the smooth feel of his suit's lining sliding around me, my arms wiggling into his sleeves. I kicked off the dress with the cheap heels and watched it settle onto the floorboard. Toed off the shoes and watched black soles and silk straps join the dress. Curled into Brett's chest and let his arms come around me, his head dropping to mine. I was dirty, he would need to burn this jacket. This truck. Everything associated with this event.

"I love you." I whispered the words that I had said a thousand times into my empty cell, imagining this moment, imagining his smell, his kiss, the desperate relief that I just saw in his eyes. I got all of those things and it took five minutes for me to remember to say *I love you.*

"Oh my God, Riley." His hands cupped underneath my bare legs, pulled me onto his lap as he inhaled my scent and placed a long kiss against my lips. "I love you too. I love you so much."

Riley. I had thought, for long nights in the cell, that I would never hear that name again. Had coveted thoughts of it, like a fantasy I was scared to indulge. I pulled at him, needed more of his kiss, more of his contact, more of the sound of my name on his lips.

Riley. Never again would I be subservient, lost, dead.

I was alive. Free. With Brett, his mouth warm and gentle against my own. My head spun as I tried to process it all. The hope I had held onto for so long… it had happened. I pulled off his mouth and gulped in air. Shook against the strength of his hands. For a moment I couldn't breathe.

Never again would I be Kitten.

CHAPTER 66
BRETT

When Elyse disappeared, I was asleep. In my home in Fort Lauderdale, I slept right through the moment when, in a nightclub, she collapsed. Most of her bachelorette party was on the upper floor of the club, drinking martinis around a private table. Elyse and her best friend left the group to go downstairs to dance. Those nearby said that Elyse collapsed on the dance floor and was taken away by a doctor and a helpful bystander, Brittany glued to her unconscious side. Everyone assumed they were taken to a hospital; only Elyse and Brittany never made it to one. They never made it anywhere. My phone rang right before dawn, a bridesmaid's voice nervously coming through the receiver. She let me know what had happened. I was on a plane within the hour. In a Mexican police station by 7 AM. Six hours too late.

That day cracked the foundation of my life, my soul. The day her body was found destroyed me, a piece of my being forever gone, lost into the cruelty that was this world. I thought, on that day, that I had experienced the worst loss of my life. That, if I ever crawled out of my hole of despair, I'd be a stronger man for it. That I'd be tougher, smarter.

Elyse's death had destroyed me. Riley's disappearance … I almost took my life in those days. Had her body turned up in the Mexican desert, I would have. The only thing that kept me alive, kept me breathing, was my mission to find and save her. I wasn't the same man who had searched for Elyse. I was smarter, more connected, savvier. I was also more ruthless.

That night, in Puerto Vallarta, when Riley had followed me – I was buying girls. Had gone – not upstairs, as Menas had mentioned to Riley – downstairs, into the basement of the club, a giant space that housed over a hundred women. I bought thirteen that night. Climbed back up the stairs, into that salsa club, proud. Happy. Glanced at my watch as I re-entered the club. It was still early. She'd be up, waiting for me. And I suddenly couldn't wait to see her. I didn't know that she was already an hour away, in the trunk of that asshole's car. I walked out of that club a naïve individual. Walked into the hotel still clueless. Didn't even understand it when I walked into an empty hotel suite, her satellite phone on the bedside table. It took me another hour to fully comprehend it, the moment when I fully accepted it … it was a punch hard into my chest, a punch that broke through bone and gripped my heart and squeezed so hard that I physically ached. I fell onto my knees in the middle of the Puerto Vallarta police station and sobbed like a child. I broke into pieces on that dirty linoleum floor. Then I called my men.

In the nine months of Riley's disappearance, I killed three men in my search for her. I wasn't proud of that fact. But trust me, they were men who deserved to die. I wanted to kill this man as well, wanted nothing more than to physically rip him apart with my hands. But that would be Riley's decision to make. I couldn't weigh her down with my sins, wouldn't burden her with the guilt that I would always carry.

Elyse's disappearance hadn't been my fault. Riley's had. I was the sole reason she was in that salsa club. The sole reason she was alone, in that dangerous country, without protection. Nine days would have been too long, much less nine months. I didn't know how to take that time back, didn't know how I would love her the rest of her life without smothering her. Because, honestly, all I wanted to do, for the rest of my life, was protect her. Never leave her side. Love her. Treasure her. Marry her. Make her smile. Hear her laugh. Love her sweetly, deeply, and into forever.

I watched her sleep and wanted to touch her, but worried I would crush her with my love.

chapter 67

Carlos Menas made it five steps out of the building, a new slave by his side, when he was taken. The girl was put into one black SUV, he in the other, accompanied by three men. Men who had spent the last four years in Brett's employ. Men who rescued a thousand girls from men like him. Men who had killed before, and put no value on his life.

At the house, an oceanfront mansion rented for the trip, Brett drew me a bath. Climbed in behind me and held me when I cried. Brought in a team of chefs, a doctor, and a masseuse, all of which were unnecessary. I wanted only to be in his arms, nothing else. The next morning, we climbed up the steps and onto his jet, heading straight home to my family. Jena had been right, sitting in my kitchen eons ago. The jet *was* twice as big, twice as luxurious as the plane I had always taken. A hundred questions and confirmations that could all wait for later. I settled into the seat, my hand in his, and didn't know. Didn't realize that back in Puerto Vallarta:

Brett's team tracked down Carlos Menas' car.

Moved him from their SUV into the trunk.

Drove him back across the border, straight to the address listed on his vehicle registration, a home thirty miles outside of Albuquerque.

Forcibly returned him to his home, leaving him chained in the basement, in a cell that had, less than 72 hours before, belonged to ~~Kitten~~ me. Then they called Brett.

We were in my parents' living room when the call came. Unbeknownst to me, Brett had become close with my family during the nine months of my capture. Had flown twenty times between Lauderdale and Quincy. Trusted my father with information he had never shared with me. Kept him apprised to the buying trips, to the slaves rescued, to the women - none of which were me. They hadn't known what had happened to me, hadn't been certain that I was taken for the slave trade, yet Brett had doubled his efforts there. My father had come to Cancun, and they had watched hotel security footage, had tracked down my helpful cabbie, had spoken to employees of the salsa club. No one remembered me, or reported sightings of the man. We had both, in the events of that night, been unmemorable enough to have never existed.

When Brett's phone rang, he glanced at the display, then at my father. I caught the look that passed, noticed the curl of my father's fingers against his pant leg when Brett stood up and excused himself, his voice low when he brought the phone to his ear. My father's leg jumped, a nervous jiggle, and I wasn't surprised when he stood up, his hurried steps carrying him outside to the patio, my eyes following them.

"Are you okay?" My mother's hand touched my arm and I jumped, my gaze skipping to her, the pained look at my response twisting my gut.

I smiled and hoped it looked normal. "Yes, Mom. I'm just glad to be home."

"God, when I think of what you must have been through..." her hand trembled when she covered her mouth and I noticed the absence of polish on her nails. She'd always worn polish, gets it done on Tuesdays after work, her standard appointment. I suddenly picked up on the other details. The grey at her roots, the dead cigarettes in the ashtray. I was gone for nine months and my mother fell apart. My heart squeezed at the realization. I reached out and clasped her hand, gripped it firmly. "It wasn't what you think, Mom. He wasn't bad.

Honestly. He was a psychology freak, liked to ask questions. That was most of it."

She swallowed and gripped my hand. Ran her other one over the top of our clasp, her cold fingers tracing the lines of my veins. "I can see your bruises, Riley. Your winces. I can hear the change in your breaths, the pain in your voice. I am, though I haven't always been the best, your mother."

I bit my bottom lip and tried not to cry. "You are the best mother I could ever want."

"No," she said softly, "but I'll try harder to be."

The kitchen door slammed shut and I looked up to see two sets of grim faces. "Riley," my father said. "Forgive my interruption, but we need to make a decision and I think you should be involved."

chapter 68

1 month after rescue

When Brett was born, he was the first of two. Two hearts, two sets of chubby hands, two kicking and screaming sets of skin that burst into the world as the two Betschart heirs — impossible babies born to a barren mother, an early miracle of in vitro before the practice was common. They spent the first ten months of their lives in a space no bigger than a basketball. And they came out inseparable. The day I met Brett, his heart was already taken. He'd given it to a six year old girl who let his GI Joes kidnap her Barbies. A fifteen-year-old who'd sacrificed her best friend to his heartbreaking ways. An eighteen-year-old high school senior who had begged him to stay local then sent him care packages every other weekend when he went to Duke. A girl who, at thirty years old, disappeared while at a friend's bachelorette party in Cancun. A girl whose remains were found two years later in the Nevada desert.

I stood at her grave and stared down at the headstone of Elyse Marine Betschart. Dug my toes against the leather of my sandals and smelled fresh-cut grass. Wondered if she smelled freedom before she died. If it was in an attempt to escape, or if she died in a cell. Wondered, in her days of pain, if she, like me, held on to thoughts of Brett.

"Let's go." Brett's fingers threaded through my own. His gentle pull brought my forehead to his lips. I closed my eyes and appreciated the moment, the tickle of my hair against my throat, the smell of him when he let go of my hand and wrapped his arms around my torso, pulled me to his chest. We stood there for a moment, the beat of his heart against my ear, the fuzz of his sweater the softest thing against my cheek I could ever imagine. I had worried, some sleepless nights in that cell, that I'd cringe from his touch. That the experiences I'd undergone would scar my psyche in ways unrecoverable. That one day I'd escape, yet always be imprisoned by that hell. My fear had lifted the first time Brett had touched me. Kissed me. Cried my name while cradling me in his arms. He was nothing like that man. His touch nothing like his bite. His words a galaxy away, his love a strength that would protect me until I died.

"Okay," I said, and let him lead me to the car.

chapter 69

3 months after rescue

"Good morning Ms. Johnson."

"Good morning."

"Welcome to Fort Lauderdale."

"Thank you." I crossed my legs, then remembered some article about it causing varicose veins, and uncrossed them. *Varicose veins.* Why the hell was I thinking about that? I smoothed a crease on my new pants. They were a size 6. I'd never worn a size 6; I'd always been more in the 12 or 14 range. But nine months of a slave's diet put me into this territory, into this body. A body I would have once killed to have and now wanted nothing to do with. I missed my curves. So did Brett. He was trying to feed me at every opportunity, yet nothing was happening. It was like my body was resistant, not letting me move past this moment in time just yet.

"Are you settled in?"

I shrugged. Looked up into the woman's eyes. "You can call me Riley."

She smiled. "Okay. Riley. You can call me Nicole."

I needed my name. Needed to hear it as much as possible. I had the irrational desire to become a teenybopper and plaster it on every surface. This morning I wrote it onto the tag of all my new clothes, like I did when I was eleven and went away to camp. Then I went down to breakfast, the scratch of my nametag comforting on my neck.

I told Brett, over eggs and potatoes, that I wanted a tattoo. The script of my name along the inside of my wrist. So I could look down at any moment and see it. So that, if I ever got taken again, I could hold up my hand and stare into his face and say "Look! I am not Kitten. I am Riley!" And never again would I wonder. And neither would anyone else.

"Are you settled in?"

She worked for Brett—this doctor. Worked for the organization that he had secretly run since Elyse died. Brett asked me to meet with her and to give him my opinion. To see if I thought she was effective and a good fit for the rescued slaves. But I knew why I was really here. And I understood that. I thought that, despite the face I showed Brett and my parents, I needed this. I reached for the glass of water on the side table. Took a sip before answering her.

"Yes, I think so. Fort Lauderdale is very different than Quincy. It's been … an adjustment. But I'm not sure if I'm adjusting more to being back in the real world, or if it's adjusting to the move."

"Why did you move so quickly? You could have stayed in Quincy longer."

I shook my head. "I … I couldn't go back to work when I got back. I just couldn't. Couldn't sit across from someone and discuss a savings account when I had just been … I tried to. But it all seemed so trivial. And without work … I just had no purpose, was just there, taking up space. And Brett was here, helping…" I straightened my shoulders. "I think it's healing. To help with the girls. It has meaning. I understand how it's helped him to heal from Elyse. And I think it will help me heal. Does that make sense?"

She leaned forward and gripped my hand. "Absolutely." She smiled sadly. "And I absolutely understand it."

I broke the eye contact and looked down at our clasped hands, noting, with a jolt of surprise, the scars on her wrists. Not that of a suicide attempt. I rolled my wrist over, the same wrist I planned to tattoo, and compared our similar handcuff scars. I squeezed her hand and looked back up to her eyes. My mouth returned her smile but inside my heart cried.

chapter 70

4 months after rescue

"Ms. Johnson, you do understand that you are here of your own free will and are under no obligation to make this statement?"

I nodded. "I do."

"I have a series of questions to ask, ones to verify the verbal statement you just provided, after which time you will write a written narrative of your events. Do you understand?"

"I do."

"On October 12th, you visited the Cendez Salsa Club in Puerto Vallarta, is that correct?"

"Yes."

"Why were you alone in the city at night?"

"I was just wasting time. Brett—my boyfriend—was having a business dinner."

"And in the salsa club you were approached by Carlos Menas who took you into a secluded area of the club and injected you with some form of drug, is that correct?"

"Yes."

"And your next memory was awakening in handcuffs and ankle shackles in the basement of his home in Albuquerque, New Mexico. Is that correct?"

"It is."

"How long were you in Mr. Menas' care?"

"I was a prisoner of Carlos Menas until I escaped about nine months later." *It would have been 268 hatchmarks.*

"And you escaped on July 7th in Puerto Vallarta, Mexico. Is that correct?"

"Yes. He had taken me there to sell me and purchase another slave."

"And you escaped his care and ran to a hotel, where you called your prior boyfriend, Brett Betschart?"

"Yes."

"And Brett Betschart just *happened* to be in the same city?"

"I was taken from there. I'm sure he made many trips there since my disappearance to look for me."

My lawyer, a suit with a Yale diploma on his wall, leaned forward, far enough to catch my eye and gave me a warning look. Oh, right. No elaborating. I forgot. I flicked my eyes back toward the man, an FBI agent.

"Why didn't you call the police upon your return to America?"

"I called my father. He's the Chief of Police in my town."

"So you called your father and told him where Mr. Menas lived?"

"Not initially. I was in shock."

"What is your understanding of what your father did with that information?"

"I believe that he went to New Mexico and coordinated with local authorities there."

"Would you be surprised to know that your father did not contact the police but instead went straight to Mr. Menas' house, where it appears he tortured the man for several days before surrendering him to police?"

"Would I be surprised?"

"Yes."

"No, I would not be surprised. But I don't know what my father did when he left Quincy." Or Brett. They left together, three days after I returned home. Three days spent in a combination of smothering me with love and grilling me about my stay. I didn't want to know what they did to him, yet a small part of me wanted every painful detail. They let him live, I knew that. They let him live and now he was in the custody of the New Mexico judicial system.

"Thank you for your cooperation, Ms. Johnson. Special Agent Haster will escort you to a private room for your written statement."

I nodded and rose. Remembered, at the last minute, that I could look him in the eye.

chapter 71

4 months, 3 weeks after rescue

I blew into the snow and it poofed, a hundred snowflakes bursting into the air, the wind sweeping a blast of them back into my face and I giggled, wiping a gloved hand over my ski mask. I looked around for Brett, the canvas of white before me blank and uninterrupted. Behind me, the glow of the cabin beckoned, the interior lights illuminating the cozy interior through the huge expanse of windows. I let out a long breath, the act frosting in the air before me, and looked up, into the night sky.

Out here, a galaxy above me, my view fringed with snow-capped branches and falling flurries, I feel— OOMPH. I stagger back, spitting out snow as I bat at my mask, the reaction futile as I am hit with another snowball, my twisting defense causing me to fall, one big awkward pile of fleece, my feet going up, gloved hands struggling to scrape at the snow, to form my own missile in which to destroy my opponent.

"Easy there," Brett's voice, his hot breath, warms my ear in the moment before he tackles me, pinning my arms and rolling with me down the slight hill. We roll to a stop, his mouth stealing a frigid kiss against an exposed patch of neck. "If you hit me with one of those, I'll be forced to withhold hot chocolate."

I dropped the partially formed snowball and held up my hands, grinning up at him. "A highly effective threat. I surrender."

"Promise?" he tilts his head at me suspiciously. "You'll be mine, forever and ever?"

"Forever and ever," I whisper. "As long as that sentence comes with hot chocolate."

His mouth twitches and he lets out a troubled sigh. "I can't promise hot chocolate..." He pushes off and offers me his hand. "But I do have this?" He pulls me to my feet, us doing a seesaw when I right and he drops, onto one knee, his other hand lifting and holding out a ring box. "Riley, will you marry me?"

When I gasp, there is a cloud of smoke, and through it I see his smile. "I can't open it with these damn gloves," he says sheepishly.

I drop to my knees before him and wrap my arms around him. "Yes," I say in a giant marshmallow hug of material. "I don't need to see it. Yes."

He squeezes me so tightly I laugh, his arms managing to lift us both up to standing. "Forever?" he asks, setting me down and stepping back, pulling me up the hill, towards the house. Through the glass, I see my girls, a few nosy ones at the window, their hands cupping the glass, Chelsea in the background holding up a champagne bottle. Brett's friends, the same men who were there the night I was rescued, are scattered throughout the room, one ... I squint ... mid-kiss with Megan? I stifle a smile and turn back to my future husband.

"Yes, Brett. Forever."

He pumps his fist in the air, and everyone inside jumps up and cheers, the muffled cry passing through the glass to us. I jog a few steps, catching up, and let him pull me against his side.

The word 'tight' has twenty-two definitions, but my favorite is Webster's fifth - "a bond which cannot be broken." We had survived secrets, suspicions, and separation, and perhaps been strengthened by all of it in some ways. Once he broke down and told me about Elyse, it all made sense. My suspicions found their answers and he found my trust. Now, we had no secrets, and a vow to never keep any. He had saved me from hell, and healed me back to life, all in less than two years. We were one unit and not only could our bond not be broken, it would only strengthen with time.

chapter 72

1 year, 5 months after rescue

I spent the last week before my imprisonment thinking that Brett was running drugs. Spent the first few months in Carlos Menas' basement of the same opinion. Somewhere, in between the sessions and the erosion of my mind, I stopped thinking about the bad and focused only on the good. I stopped caring whether Brett was involved in an illegal drug ring and started caring only about us. Whether our love was strong enough. Whether he would love me for me. Whether the teeth that had been pulled from my jaw reached him and my father or whether they simply settled into the kitchen trash of Menas' home, a lesson in psychology and nothing more.

The police did find my teeth in their search of his home. They were bagged, tagged, and put in neat order next to the other exhibits. Photos of me. Recordings. My sketches. My early journal entries. Everything laid out in perfect organization next to his interviews. It made a stunning exhibit at his trial.

Carlos Menas ended up getting a twenty-four year sentence. He will be released from prison around his seventieth birthday. Brett, to this day, curses himself for not killing the man.

I moved to south Florida a month or so after my rescue, much to the chagrin of my friends. I am happy here, happy anywhere that is in arms reach of this man. I now work in the rehabilitation house, with the slaves that Brett rescues. I can relate to these women, can understand their struggle. Am taking classes in psychology in hopes of helping them more. My father, after being cleared from charges of assault against Menas, has also joined the rescue business. He works with law enforcement, feeding them information we are gleaning from the girls, and they are taking down as many of the trafficking operations as possible. While Brett's practices might be frowned upon in the States, the Central American countries are turning a blind eye to any questionable methods, and accepting our funding and information with open arms. To date, we've taken down five traders and - with Brett's previous tally included - saved over twelve hundred women. It will never be enough, there will always be monsters, there will always be missing women. But it is the best therapy I could ever have, the best use of my life I could ever wish for.

A part of me died in that cell, in my life as Kitten.

But another part of me was born. Grew. Held onto the love in my heart and fought back, was freed, became a woman who married a man. A woman who reclaimed her life. And today, at 2:21 PM, a woman who gave birth to a baby girl. I look down at my new purpose in life and smile. Gently squeeze her against my chest and feel the sigh of her breath. Our baby. Elyse Riley Betschart. I glance over at my husband and see the fear in his eyes. His level of love scares him. Our happiness scares him. He has gone so long with loss that I don't think he knows how not to fear, how not to worry. I reach out my hand and he grabs it. Holds it tight.

THE END

Want to be notified when Alessandra's next book releases?
Visit www.nextnovel.com

Author's Note:

Oh my word. TIGHT is now my ninth novel. And I've never struggled with a novel like I did with it. I experienced, in these pages, my first ever writer's block. Ended up rewriting the book three times, with three different plot lines and outcomes! I just couldn't fit the pieces in place. Then, they finally did. I worried that they wouldn't. They kept me stressing up into the very end.

I think the hardest thing was the fact that I first published Still - a novella with Brett and Riley. That novella created them in the reader's mind, solidified them as the people that they were at that moment in time. I couldn't really change their characters once I went and published them. So... it was like my hands were tied, and I had to find my way back to the place that my mind was at when I first wrote that novella. When I finally found that place, I really tried to write a contemporary romance, one without twists and turns and deceit. But... yeah. My mind and my characters didn't behave and TIGHT was born.

I write this author's note to you only ten days before release. And tomorrow, I will start a new book, one whose storyline is already breathing down my neck. Want to know more? Go to http://www.nextnovel.com to be notified by email when I have a new release!

If this is your first book from me, please know that this book is a little different from my others. Thank you for picking up Tight, I hope that you enjoyed it and will share it with your friends.

This book did not grow to its full potential on its own. Thank you SueBee, Wendy Metz, Karen Lawson and Marion Archer for beta reading this baby through all of its rewrites! Your level of patience and attention to this book was admirable. Thank you Julie Kitzmiller and Sandra Anderson for reading the final version and pushing it further. Thank you Perla Calas and Janice Berry – you guys ran through the final version with a fine-toothed comb and weeded out all of my mistakes. An extra kudos to Perla for pointing out plot holes and tighten loose ends! And a giant thank you to Madison Seidler, my fabulous editor, for holding my hand and pushing the edges of this book and letting it stretch to its full potential. Thank you Keelie "Kiki" Chatfield for pimping me and my books all day, every day. Your support and marketing have spread my works to so many readers, thank you a million times over. Judi Perkins, thank you for designing amazing teasers and a kick ass cover that perfectly communicates what I wanted. Thank you Michelle Tan, Michelle New and Jx PinkLady, you guys made incredible works of art that perfectly showcased this book - thank you so much for lending me some of your graphic brilliance. And Tricia Crouch, thank you thank you thank you for your lists and organization and support and graphics and friendship and cards and for keeping me in line and on schedule, you are the best assistant a girl could ask for. Thank you Maura Kye-Casella, my incredible agent, for your constant support and for opening doors I could never get to on my own.

And last but not least, thank you to the hundreds of bloggers who tirelessly promote this industry - you are all amazing and I appreciate every single one of you!

With love,
Alessandra

***

www.alessandratorre.com
www.facebook.com/AlessandraTorre0/
www.twitter.com/ReadAlessandra
www.pinterest.com/atorreauthor/

Made in the USA
Lexington, KY
19 June 2015